CyberServed
MINE TO KEEP

By

Tracy St. John

NOTE: If you purchased this book without a cover you should be aware that this book is stolen property. The author has not received any payment for this 'stripped book'.

© copyright April 2022, Tracy St. John
Cover art by Erin Dameron-Hill, © copyright February 2022

This is a work of fiction. All characters, events, and places are of the author's imagination and not to be confused with fact. Any resemblance to living persons or events is merely coincidence.

OTHER BOOKS BY TRACY ST. JOHN

The Font
Unholy Union
To Protect and Service: Ravenous Virtue
To Protect and Service: Righteous Fury

THE CLANS OF KALQUOR

Alien Embrace
Alien Rule
Alien Conquest
Alien Salvation
Alien Slave
Alien Interludes: Clans of Kalquor Short Stories
Alien Redemption
Alien Refuge
Alien Caged
Alien Indiscretions
Alien Hostage
Alien Revolt
Alien Outcast

CLAN BEGINNINGS

To Clan and Conquer
Clan and Conviction
Clan, Honor, and Empire
Clan and Crown
Clan and Command
Clan and Conscience
Clan and Commit
Clan and Covenant

FIRST MATARAS

Michaela
Maryam
Iliana

OTHER CLANS OF KALQUOR BOOKS:

Clans of Europa: Sister Katherine
Clans of Europa: Tina
Clan Companions: Joseph
Clan Companions: Gabriel
Shalia's Diary Books 1-12

WARRIORS OF RISNAR

Not of this World
Worlds Apart
Worlds Collide
Worlds Away

NETHERWORLD

Drop Dead Sexy
Blood Potion No. 9
Once Bitten Twice Dead
Animal Attraction

CYBERSERVED

Made to Order
Mine to Keep
Built to Last

Please visit Tracy's website at: http://www.tracystjohn.com
and Tracy's blog at:
http://tracystjohn.blogspot.com

Follow on Twitter @TracySaintJohn

Chapter One

Lillian Kwolek failed to notice the protestors until she set her shuttle down in the landing bay. Then they came from seemingly everywhere and swarmed around her vessel.

"Great. Just fucking great." CyberServe's security had majorly screwed up. Demonstrators shouldn't have been able to access the shuttle bay. The company's lobby had been designated the official area for dissenters to gather, with visitors being routed through other entrances. The arrangement kept the Interplanetary Trade and Commerce System, commonly referred to as the ITCS, content. It kept Lillian Kwolek, president of CyberServe, very happy.

She spotted familiar features within the swarm of sign-waving protestors and groaned. Gunnar Jax was the leader of the Freedom League, an Earth-based movement. His scraggly beard, along with wild, unkempt hair and crooked-tooth smile, somehow failed to detract from fine-boned good looks. Not that Lillian would ever consider him attractive. Gunnar looked as he usually did; as if he'd just rolled out of a garbage reclamation unit wearing a bigger man's clothes.

For all his disreputable appearance, he was no one to screw with. Bad things had a tendency to happen when he and his people showed up. If Gunnar was there...

Of course. Artemis Neera was present as well. Her bushy brown hair was as wild as Gunnar's. Thick brows grew low over her burning eyes. Gunnar's girlfriend was a supposed founder of the Freedom League. She eschewed the spotlight, but she was always in the thick of the action. She was rumored to be among the most violent of the faction. Like Gunnar, the police had yet to make any charges of illegal activities stick to her.

Lillian reached for her phone to call security. No need. They burst into the bay, a dozen men and women shouting at the demonstrators as they waved shock batons.

Gunnar yelled in return. Inside her soundproof Strobe XL-Six, Lillian couldn't hear his or any other shouts. Most of the crowd turned and rushed the guards.

"Shit, shit, shit," Lillian groaned as she watched through the shuttle's front monitor. If any of CyberServe's employees lost his or her temper, if someone got hurt...

She put her hands to her face. Her fingers spread to allow her to peer between them as the two groups shoved each other. The situation looked as if it would go to hell in a hurry.

Should she go out there? As president of the company, she had to do something. Several demonstrators, including Neera, had remained behind to watch her craft. They obviously waited for her to put in an appearance. While Lillian had no trouble putting her fist in someone's mug, Freedom League members were renowned for fighting dirty.

Hell, Freedom League members had killed those they'd disagreed with.

The pushing and shouting grew more violent. The shock batons pointed. That only appeared to enrage to demonstrators, and they shoved harder than ever. The shit was about to hit the fan.

The double doors security had entered through opened. At least two dozen Walls and Wardens came out, and the angry tide swirled back as expressions went from rage-filled to terrified.

"Yeah, that's going to get them on our side," Lillian muttered, but she was glad to see the cyborgs marching in three columns.

The Walls...more accurately, the TWMs and TWFs...looked like their nicknames. Male and female cyborgs that bulged muscle, their brutish visages cold with intent, they'd been the big guns of the corporate wars on Earth. They'd terrorized rival corporations' cyborgs and the humans caught in the middle.

The PSMs were smaller and outfitted with less coarse features. One could call the all-male Warden models handsome with their refined physical characteristics. Nonetheless, anyone who'd spent prison time under their merciless care wouldn't acknowledge them as humane creatures. The Wardens had taken torture to horrific levels.

Many, if not all, of the Freedom League had been on Earth during the wars. They'd watched the cyborgs tear the world apart. They'd witnessed them visit atrocities on loved ones. They'd seen the cyborgs kill. Some had been personally hurt by the manufactured soldiers. A few may have been part of the desperate alliance that had finally overcome the corporations and their cyborgs. By then, Earth had damned few resources remaining, thanks to the corporate executives' greed that had turned into a free-for-all grab for riches and power.

Cyborg armies had been the terrors of Earth's corporate wars. Rather than disassemble them, cash-desperate Earth had sold the defunct salvaged remainder afterward to CyberServe. The company Lillian presided over refurbished, reprogrammed, and sold the cyborgs as devoted servants to the humans who lived off-world.

Hence the Freedom League's displeasure with Lillian's company. They'd left Earth to make their ire known in person by showing up in large crowds at CyberServe.

Lillian was delighted they were in full retreat at the moment. With the cyborg arrivals, shuttles in the visitors' slots were lifting off and flying haphazardly in their mad dash to escape. It was a wonder they avoided smashing into employees' vessels, walls, or the ceiling of the cavernous space.

By the time she stepped out of her Strobe and emerged in the midst of the cyborg phalanx, the Freedom League was gone. Torn signs, placards of hate printed in blood red, lay scattered on the bay floor.

"Good job, gang." She looked at her protectors with mingled pride and relief.

"Thank you, Mr. Kwolek," they chorused.

The very human Security Chief Scott Michaels trotted up. "I'm sorry you walked into that, Mr. Kwolek. They arrived barely a minute before you did, and I was calling in the team to turn them out when you landed. No excuse for the delay, I understand, and my resignation will be on your desk within the hour." His voice caught halfway through his speech, but the red-faced man powered through it.

Lillian took in his trim physique in his gray CyberServe security uniform. How much of his tone came from actual workouts and how much from contouring? No matter. Whether his body was real or surgically enhanced, Michaels' other qualifications were topnotch, the best she'd been able to hire when it became apparent CyberServe would have safety concerns against outside agitators.

"You most certainly won't resign, Mr. Michaels. What you'll do is figure out how those people got past the defensive grid to gain access to what should have been a fortified area. You'll fix it immediately." She eyed him severely.

The tension vacated his features, which had been allowed to show some of his middle-aged years. At least Michaels wasn't erasing the lines in his forehead or around his eyes, the way so many did. A grateful smile didn't break through, but it teased the corners of his mouth.

"Absolutely, Mr. Kwolek. Thank you. Until we figure out how those protestors got through, there'll be a full security complement guarding the bay."

"Excellent. I recognized members of the Freedom League, so you'll want to call in the regular police."

Michaels paled. "Right away." He hurried to the detail he'd brought in and barked orders.

A TWF stepped forward. Her heavy brow made her look as if she were scowling to the untrained eye. It was actually her most deadpan expression. "A detail of four was instructed to escort you to your office, Mr. Kwolek."

"Thank you, TWF."

The cyborg snapped a nod. She jerked a motion with a beefy arm. Wrapped around a human head, that arm would crush the skull like an eggshell. "Detail, assemble. All others, return to your berths and power down until needed again."

Three other cyborgs joined her in surrounding Lillian. The rest marched out ahead of them. Their boots echoed in the bay in thunderous booms.

The cyborgs were impressive. Fearsome. But thanks to Lillian, no longer deadly.

* * * *

Alek knew the soft tread of Lillian's step, and he turned to greet her as she entered her office. She left the guard detail outside her door, which closed behind her.

Assessment: Lillian Kwolek appears tense and ill-humored. Experience dictates this unit display a low-level concern approach.

After a year of functioning and learning, Alek's matrix wasn't required to tell him how to cope with Lillian. Nevertheless, it was good to have a scientific appraisal of her state of mind. "Good morning, Mr. Kwolek. I trust the ambush in the shuttle bay didn't inconvenience you too greatly?"

"It would have been far worse if you hadn't sent in the cyborgs. Good call. Thank you, Alek."

"I'm pleased to have been of service." He gave a stock answer humans expected to hear. Alek was pleased about nothing. He was also never irritated, peeved, or upset. He simply was.

He watched as Lillian slung her carrycase on the top of her polished desk. Her spiky silver hair, its ends tipped in black and red, was its usual artfully messy state. Her tie matched its coloring in alternating stripes, as did her long fingernails, which tapped nervously on her desk.

Lillian was unlike her contemporaries in many ways. Alek found her defiant non-corporate style interesting, but not enough to ask her about it. Despite the hair, which could change color daily, weekly, or monthly depending on her whims, she tended toward more of a natural look. She might go in for body contouring every month or two, depending on whether she had put on a few extra pounds, but she wasn't rabid about it. Indeed, she was a far cry from the current trend of looking like a svelte gym maven. Her shape was a top-heavy hourglass. Alek had noted the gazes of most men and quite a few women went to her ample bosom, like moths attracted to a flame. Her breasts were impressive, he supposed.

He should know. He'd seen them close up and naked. He'd mauled and sucked them numerous times. He'd even fucked her cleavage, those impressive mounds pressed together to enfold his erect cock.

She eschewed most makeup, because she preferred her rose-beige skin bare. Mascara, lip gloss, and the occasional swipe of blush when she had to make a public appearance were her sole concessions. She was a dichotomy inside and out, the most interesting human in Alek's existence.

Which wasn't saying much. Fortunately, Alek wasn't programmed to get bored. He simply existed.

Lillian sank into her chair. She drew a deep breath, perhaps to steady the tremor in her voice. "I need to report to Tosha Cameron. More importantly, I need to get her guidance on what steps to take."

"Mr. Michaels' expertise isn't adequate?" Alek's tone was modulated to imply interest.

"It may be, but as Life Tech's CEO, Mr. Cameron has been the target of attacks and assassination attempts. Her cyborg bodyguard knows more about personal security than a hundred Scott Michaels. I want their insight."

Her remark lit a few of Alek's circuits with what humans would have termed fascination. Brick, the TWM owned by Tosha Cameron, was a fully sentient cyborg with emotions. Little impressed Alek, but he found Brick's development from a basic automaton to a fully realized entity absorbing.

"May I observe your conversation?"

Lillian waved him over. "Since company protocols keep me from recording it, you'd better. She always has a laundry list of advice, and I'll never remember it all."

Alek hurried over as she sent the request for a video conference with the owner and CEO of the company that owned CyberServe.

As Lillian waited to be patched through…Tosha Cameron's aide Amadis Dubois had said the CEO wanted to speak to Lillian as soon as she finished with the call she was on…she regarded her own assistant. She needed a distraction, and Alek was a better diversion than anything else in the room.

PSM-426021, better known as Alek for the last year, was a handsome version of his model, the Warden. Lillian had experimented with his looks for six months until arriving at his current appearance. The PSMs were masculine without the heavy brows and jaws that made the TWMs so brutish. They were handsome, with none of the sleek delicacy of the Infiltrator-class cyborgs. Thanks to Lillian's upgrades, Alek approached fashion model perfection.

She'd kept the military cut of his hair because it suited him so well, but she'd changed it from a nondescript brunette to a sandy blond. She'd liked his tawny eyes, so she'd kept those. His features had been altered slightly. Lillian had directed its change from the kindly angelic cast that had been such a lie for the PSMs to reflect a firmer, no-nonsense attitude. Alek still look as if he could be an angel, but more along the lines of the avenging type.

When Lillian had discovered him among the other decommissioned cyborgs stored in a warehouse, his skin had been torn in several places, his metal skeletal limbs bent. His left arm had been completely torn off. Still, he'd been in better shape than most, and it hadn't taken long to repair him and replace the matrix that served as his brain. He wasn't the muscled behemoth that characterized the physiques of the TWMs and TWFs, but he was the sort of buff that would cost a human thousands of dollars to achieve and hundreds a year to maintain in a contouring studio.

It was what was between Alek's legs that gave him what counted in Lillian's view. The PSMs had been originally outfitted to terrorize prisoners, male and female alike, in ways she refused to imagine. Now programmed to offer pleasure instead of torture, Alek could be properly appreciated for his substantial gift.

Lillian hadn't taken him home in a couple of weeks, and she had a new upgrade to test. One of the perks of being a senior engineer for CyberTech had been bringing her 'work' home. As president, Lillian was granted even more leeway.

New upgrade or no, she deserved a satisfying fuck after the bullshit she'd encountered in the shuttle bay. The kind of demanding fuck where she couldn't think of anything except what was going on at the moment.

Her ruminations halted as Tosha Cameron's lovely face filled her viewscreen. "Mr. Kwolek, it's good to see you. What's this report about you being threatened?"

Lillian loved that about her boss: straight to the point. The lady didn't screw around.

She matched Cameron's lack of equivocation with her own. In less than a minute, Lillian laid out the facts of what had occurred in the shuttle bay and ended with a request for advice.

"After all, you know a thing or two about fending off personal attacks." She forced her tone into lightness.

Cameron chuckled. "I do. I'm glad the situation escalated no further than it did and you're safe and sound. Brick, you're the expert on these matters. What's your take?"

The holoscreen monitor widened to show Brick, Cameron's cyborg bodyguard and lover. The TWM's crude features had been softened at his request. He'd been made over into action-star delicious. Lillian got a thrill looking at him, but not just because he was a gorgeous view. Brick had been then cash-strapped CyberServe's first sale. Cameron's purchase of him had led to a partnership between CyberServe and the mega trillion-dollar Life Tech enterprise. Later, Life Tech had bought the company outright and Cameron appointed Lillian its president.

Brick's green eyes usually twinkled with humor, but he looked far from amused as he joined the conversation. "First of all, I'm delighted you're all right, Mr. Kwolek."

"Thank you, Brick."

"I hope you won't mind if Life Tech's security chief and I confer with CyberServe's Mr. Michaels after this episode."

"By all means. You'll find Mr. Michaels is easy to work with. He was recognized in his previous job for welcoming assistance from others."

"Excellent. A non-territorial chief of security is difficult to find. We'll figure out how to keep you and your employees safe. In the meantime, are you still using that PSM as an assistant?"

"Alek is right here." Lillian waved her cyborg in.

"Good morning, Mr. Brick. In what way may I be of service?" Alek stood behind Lillian.

"It would be advisable for you to download the full security program available to the cyborgs. Or, if Mr. Kwolek prefers, another cyborg can serve in the same bodyguard capacity for her as I do for Mr. Cameron."

For some reason, unease stabbed Lillian. "Do you really think that's necessary? I mean, it was chance that my shuttle landed so soon after the protestors' arrival. They probably weren't after me specifically."

"I disagree. The fact they showed up just before you and before CyberServe's security staff could remove them makes me think the confrontation was orchestrated. There may have been someone watching when you departed your home this morning. They would have tipped the others off as to when to be ready for your arrival."

"We're talking about the Freedom League. Such a ruse would fit with their modus operandi," Alek remarked.

"I can't recommend a bodyguard cyborg highly enough," Cameron chimed in. "There's a reason so many company executives are ordering them. Between that and our people getting with your head of security, you'll be in good shape for the Freedom League's next move. That bunch is tenacious, so they'll be back."

"No doubt." Lillian almost bit her lip. She sighed instead. With presidential perks came headaches, and she'd realized she'd have to expect some inconveniences when she'd accepted the position.

Inconveniences? Seriously? I call bullshit on that, Lillian.

She ignored the disbelieving voice in her head. "All right, Mr. Cameron, I appreciate the suggestions. I'll tell Mr. Michaels to expect your call, Mr. Brick."

After the call ended, Lillian regarded Alek. He gazed back. She could probably stare at him until the end of time, and he'd only stand there and wait.

Alek as her bodyguard. It made sense, no matter how part of her rebelled against the idea of letting anyone…even an emotionless cyborg…spend too much time close to her. Yet Brick and Cameron were right. The Freedom League had left Earth to take up the anti-cyborg cause, and as CyberServe's president, Lillian would be their focus.

She fought off a shudder.

Alek was no Brick as far as strength was concerned, but the Warden was as resilient as any Wall. Putting her unfounded concerns aside, he was the obvious choice to serve as her bodyguard. If she could be said to trust anyone, it was Alek.

"Thoughts?" she prompted him.

"As always, I'm at your service. I am ready to assume the task of your personal security if you desire me to do so."

"Well, it would keep you close at hand for other tasks. I planned on taking you home tonight for some research. I guess we'll make it a more regular thing until we figure out how to discourage the Freedom League." Spoken in her breeziest tone.

Nothing to see here, folks. It was no big deal.

"Download the full security program?" Alek was only interested in the task to be accomplished.

Lillian drew a breath. "Download."

"Full download will be completed in five minutes."

"Great. You do that, and I'll get to work. Freedom League or not, I have a full schedule today." She tapped on her computer and scowled at nothing in particular. "I should have stayed in R and D."

Her day wasn't merely full. It was wall-to-wall, with a schedule that would have been impossible without Alek's organizational skills. When Lillian had taken the job, she'd known Alek would outperform any human executive assistant. There'd been no point in hiring anyone else.

That was the reason other dissenters without the Freedom League's agenda of vengeful justice gathered in protest against CyberServe. They were afraid the cyborgs would take their jobs.

A valid concern for the far-off future, because cyborgs were remarkably adaptable to whatever was needed. If CyberServe lacked a career's program, its cyborgs could still learn tasks at a phenomenal rate.

It wasn't Lillians' job to worry about such things. As the situation currently stood, cyborgs were too expensive for most individuals and companies to afford. Jobs were safe from their taking over in the foreseeable future.

She scowled at her workload and mentally vowed she wouldn't stay late in the office. Lillian wanted to play with her latest sex program. Cyborgs for sex were all the rage among the ultrarich at the moment. Fortunately, the 'we're not getting laid because of cyborgs' protest contingent hadn't yet formed to harass Lillian.

As she went over the latest sales charts, she considered what her night with Alek held in store. Lillian was an unapologetic mechasexual, a human who accepted only cyborgs as sexual partners. Alex had been her first, and thus far, was still the best she'd taken home. Though such dalliances were as impersonal as a hired dick, at least Lillian no longer had to pay to score her jollies.

Otherwise, it would be a menage of me, myself, and I.

No human men. No romantic entanglements. She'd learned her lesson where that was concerned. Life was on the lonely side, especially with her at the helm of CyberServe. Being its president took up far more of her time than her job as an engineer had, but at least she didn't have to worry about being hurt.

"Security program has completed downloading," Alek said.

She glanced at him. "How do you feel?"

"The matrix says I'm operating within system parameters."

Good old Alek. Unlike the human race, he gave her nothing to worry about.

Everywhere he looked, Alek saw threats.

The door to the office locked automatically, but it wasn't reinforced. He could have punched through it easily, which meant any cyborg in the wrong hands could also be ordered to do so. Though the new protocols should inhibit any cyborg ordered to commit harm to a human, there were always methods the programmers might have missed.

Certain weapons could break through too. Those sorts of weapons would be in the hands of the military only, but again, exceptions could never be discounted.

There were no other accesses to Lillian's office. That should have soothed the watchfulness the security program had given Alek, but instead, it worried him more. She'd be cornered if someone with harmful intent broke in. And what of a fire? How would she escape dangers beyond those of murderous demonstrators?

This new program has presented me with uncomfortable insights, he told his matrix.

Lillian Kwolek is no less safe than she was before this unit added the security protocol to the system. There is still the automatic security field and two guarded checkpoints between all headquarters accesses and her office.

Yes, but I wasn't so aware of the issues before now.

He considered his options. The first was obvious. "Mr. Kwolek, will you grant me full access to CyberServe's security system?"

She was frowning at her computer and didn't bother to look in his direction. "Yeah, sure. Connect with Mr. Michaels and start the ball rolling on whatever you need for your assignment. Let me know what you require me to approve."

Alek obeyed. He simultaneously conversed with his matrix as he alerted Michaels to the incoming request and the reason for it. He also sent Lillian a batch of forms and reviewed the next few days' schedules with her protection in mind.

My data on Brick explains that his initial moves into sentience and emotion came about with the addition of his interpersonal relations program to the security program he began with.

His matrix: *Accurate.*

Other life assistants have also reportedly achieved these advancements. I have an interpersonal program already active, to which Lillian has added the advanced security module. Should I anticipate emotional awareness?

The answer arrived without a second's pause. *This matrix is unfamiliar with the details of unit Brick's evolution to emotional maturity. I cannot answer this unit's question with reliable accuracy.*

Can the matrix extrapolate a theory?

Certain fully upgraded programs, including the interpersonal software, can spur true emotions.

My interpersonal software is basic, not advanced. Am I safe from emotional distress?

This unit has achieved self-awareness and learned much over the past year of its operation. Over time, emotions may naturally occur. Should this unit wish to accelerate the process, the matrix advises it to request an upgrade to its interpersonal programming, as it is that software which seems to offer best emotional growth.

Alek weighed the suggestion for barely an instant before dismissing it. He had no interest in gaining emotions. From what he'd seen of the cyborgs that had developed such curious tics, they appeared less focused on their appropriate functions. Even Brick was occasionally unprofessional in Mr. Cameron's presence. The TWM cracked jokes and discussed dinner plans when the *mood* hit him. Like Alek, he could pay close attention to several matters at once, but the mere appearance of distraction was enough to make Alek wish to put off any disruptions that might leave Lillian unguarded.

Speaking of which, he had information to gather.

For the next hour, he researched Gunnar Jax, the face and leader of the Freedom League. What he found gave him pause.

"From now on, you don't go anywhere without me," Alek informed Lillian.

Her gaze shifted from her computer to him. "Is that the program talking or you? Because I'm less than crazy about that tone."

Chapter Two

Alek ignored Lillian's warning. He had bigger concerns. "Have you researched this Gunnar Jax you noted among the protestors?"

"Not really. A little. I know he's in charge of an organization that's been big trouble to Earth since they emerged from the corporation wars. He hates cyborgs because he was in the middle of that crazy shit."

"More than in the middle. He was drowning in it. His city was occupied early in the conflict by the energy conglomerate Powertech, which was local. In fact, his father worked for it. When Jax was ten, rival corporation Solarcorp attacked with an army of cyborgs and grabbed control for a short time."

"An army of cyborgs? He saw that?"

"That and much worse. Men and women were raped by the cyborgs…in their homes, in stores, in the streets, wherever the Walls and the Wardens decided a demonstration should be made. Gunnar's own father was beaten to death in front of him as they scrounged for scraps in a refuse bin."

Lillian stared at him, her expression horrified. "Jupiter's storm, Alek. Where did you get that information from?"

"Jax's autobiography. You can download it off the cyber grid. I've cross-checked and verified he was in the area during that particular period of conflict. I've also confirmed the circumstances under which his father was killed and found multiple witnesses who corroborate Jax's version of the events."

"I think I'm gonna be sick."

"Jax alleges that when Powertech's cyborg army initially brought the fight to his neighborhood, he was pinned in an alley by the crossfire. He spent nearly two days hiding inside a garbage dumpster while the battle raged."

"He was ten years old then?"

"Yes. When he was twelve, which was the last year of the wars, local rebels forced him to run messages to allied forces across town. He was cornered by a PSM...my model. The Warden took aim and was about to kill him when a freedom fighter group hit it with a grenade and saved his life. Are you all right, Mr. Kwolek?"

Lillian had turned corpse-pale. "Hell no, I'm not all right. He grew up in a warzone, for fuck's sake."

Alek gazed at her and wondered at her surprise. Surely she knew Earth's recent history despite being a "starkid," someone born within the ITCS' group of space stations. The corporate wars had been over for only thirty years.

"He grew up under those circumstances until the FPC gained control, formed the current government, and put the leaders and board executives of the corporations on trial."

"What happened afterward on Earth was barely better, wasn't it? Starvation, disease. They're still struggling." One of CyberServe's long-term goals was to send in cyborgs to help repair Earth's infrastructure...very far in the future, due to the Terran population's horrific history with the cyborgs. As desperate as their situation was, those living on Earth repulsed any offer that included their former antagonists' return.

"It's an ugly situation but slowly improving. They don't have to worry about my kind marching in and destroying their lives any longer."

"You're so matter-of-fact about it," Lillian sighed.

"It's regrettable how cyborgs were used to terrorize humans just so a few companies could plunder resources. But no, I feel nothing over what was done. I don't have that capacity."

"Be grateful. Past regrets are no fun to deal with."

They'd strayed from the topic, and Alek brought them back. "Gunnar Jax met his lover Artemis Neera when they were in their mid-twenties. She had already begun the fledging group that eventually became the Freedom League, which protested what they believed was the coddling of the former executive class and its military leaders."

"If weekly executions can be called coddling." Lillian snorted.

"There were a few spared the firing squads and hangings, mostly because the FPC was interrogating them about the locations of where they'd hidden resources, weapons, and the like. Death sentences were commuted to life imprisonment in exchange for freely offered information."

"Which pissed off a large number of people who'd been victimized by the corporations."

"Radicalization of a certain mindset was a given."

"Jax being among the recruited. He somehow became the face of the Freedom League," Lillian noted.

"It happened when he insulted a peacekeeper at a protest attended by himself and Neera. And when I say he insulted the officer, I mean he screamed in the man's face nonstop. The officer finally lashed out and whacked Jax with a baton. Jax's bloody face, with him raising his fist in defiance as other sentries dragged his attacker off, transformed into a rallying cry. The Freedom League's membership went into overdrive, and it was the biggest anti-clemency group within a couple of weeks."

Lillian considered. "It almost sounds as if the encounter was planned. As if Jax wanted to come under attack."

Alek offered her a smirk that his basic interaction program said was appropriate. "Doesn't it?"

"What about the death count I've heard tell of? Freedom League has a pretty bloody past from what little I've gathered."

"It's quite large, even if you discount the supposed executions. Most notably, members of the Freedom League famously caused the Alexandria Prison Riot ten years ago, in which inmates grabbed control of the facility. Instead of attempting to escape, they locked their guards in cells and let in twenty agitators."

Lillian had heard only a few details of the incident. "Go on."

"Three former corporate executives who'd had a hand in the wars were incarcerated in Alexandria. They'd cooperated with the new government to have their executions commuted to life sentences. The Freedom League prisoners and agitators put them on mock trial, found them guilty, and hanged them. Jax wasn't there, but he supposedly masterminded the whole thing, though no one could find evidence or gain testimony against him."

"That wasn't the only occasion his followers took the legal hit for Freedom League-related attacks."

"They're apparently willing to suffer the consequences for his sake. It doesn't matter how many people he loses through incarceration. Every attack brings more people into his organization."

"Now he and his cult have left Earth and come out here because he hates cyborgs. This could turn ugly, Alek."

He regarded her steadily. "Which is why I'm now your bodyguard. As I said, you won't be leaving my sight from now on."

Why did Alek's statement send a thrill up her spine?

After a moment, Lillian identified the delicious shiver's source: he looked as he did when they had sex. When he was playing the part of master to her slave. Determined. Focused. Don't-fuck-with-me-or-you'll-get-it control.

Except this time, she didn't have to work at believing it. Alek wasn't playing a part she'd assigned. He meant it.

"Sir, yes sir," she retorted. She pretended the crotch of her panties hadn't just become soaked.

Alek snorted and returned his attention to his computer. She guessed that meant their conversation about Gunnar Jax was over. But Mr. Power Play had reminded her about the bondage program she wanted to try out.

Lillian had a very particular bent when it came to sex, beyond lusting for the nonhuman. Thanks to cyborgs, she had no need to vet men to find the perfect playmates for her other kinks.

She liked sex with an edge. Which was hilarious. She was such a chicken in most avenues of life. She was claustrophobic and terrified of heights. She piloted her shuttle slightly below the speed limit. Refused to shake hands for fear of catching viruses, and when illnesses started going around, she was the first to wear a mask.

But give a cyborg a paddle, cuffs, and clamps, and she was primed to go crazy. She lived for the adrenaline high and endorphin rush that apprehension and pain offered.

She licked her lips and thought about the night she had planned. Alek would put her in her place, whether it be on her knees or splayed on whatever horizontal surface seemed particularly inviting. Or up against a wall. Bless cyborgs and their strength that allowed them to support a woman's weight with ease.

And bless them for being unfeeling not-men.

* * * *

MINE TO KEEP

Lillian's three-bedroom condo in Sector G of Alpha Station was a modest little home. Certainly, it wasn't the palatial penthouse most successful company presidents lived in, with large spaces built for entertaining, swimming pools, observatories, gardens the size of parks, or anything of that nature.

She could have afforded such a place, but much like refusing to contouring herself into the latest body trend, ostentatiousness wasn't her style. Lillian preferred coziness over luxury, comfort over fashion. She had indulged in a little redecorating when her salary soared, but her home remained simple.

She entered it at the end of her day with the same sense of relief she usually felt. Chewing the last bite of a chicken and vegetable wrap she'd picked up for dinner on her way home, she was barely through the door when she kicked her shining black oxfords off her feet and plunged her silver-painted toenails into the deep pile carpet. She sighed.

Alek brushed past her after ensuring the door was locked. He immediately began examining every closet, corner, and room.

"I have an alarm system, you know. If anyone was here, there'd be security swarming all over the place," she called after him.

"Unless it was a security specialist breaking in. That's how the Freedom League has managed to infiltrate several targets. They actively train their people to circumvent defensive systems." Alek's voice faded as he swept through the condo.

"There's no one in here. Chill out." When he ignored her, Lillian muttered, "I need the systems department to test that program for paranoia." She tugged her tie loose and left the foyer for the great room.

The dining, kitchen, and television areas were all part of a single large space. The kitchen, in chrome and indigo, was spotless. Lillian did her cooking for the week during the weekend, so she could walk in the door and heat her dinner in a minute. Workdays tended to run late, so she was eager to eat the instant she got home.

With her libido running hot, she'd grabbed her dinner to go so she could get down to fun as soon as she reached her condo. However, Alek was playing bodyguard, which put her plans on hold. She grumbled under her breath and tossed her suit jacket and tie over the back of her overstuffed sofa.

She gazed at the television room's fireplace and contemplated ordering it to light. But Alek couldn't possibly take long to verify the condo didn't have any bogeymen waiting to jump out at her. There was no point in having a fire when they would spend most of the night in the playroom.

A smile tugged at her lips as she thought of the extra bedroom she'd outfitted for sex. No, she'd not be hanging around the soft blue-and-cream television room tonight. Her environs would be black walls and mirrors, and the sounds snapping leather and cries, rather than the crackle of flames.

She turned toward the hall that led to the rest of the home as Alek emerged from it to stand in front of her. His demeanor surprised her. He appeared confrontational.

"I fail to see my actions as a representation of paranoia given what my research revealed of Gunnar Jax and the Freedom League."

"I can't believe you heard that offhand remark halfway across the apartment. You don't think you're going a bit overboard?" Her tone was teasing.

"When you consider the number of attacks, beatings, and hangings that we know of and the numerous missing of their enemies, it should give you pause. Have you seen these pictures?" He held up his personal tablet. The screen depicted a scene so horrific, Lillian's mind refused to understand it at first. "This is the politician they targeted after she advocated to release one former senior advisor from Powertech due to lack of evidence of personal involvement. Her blackened corpse sitting in her car, right there in her driveway—"

"Shut up, Alek." All visions of sweaty sex were driven from Lillian's mind by the awful image. Her fantasies were replaced by visions of her arrival in CyberServe's shuttle bay: the hectic, fanatical light in Jax's eyes, the bald hatred of Neera's scowl. Would they have set fire to her shuttle with her in it if help hadn't come? The idea added to the cold, creeping fear Lillian had kept at bay during the day with distractions of work and plans for the night. Terror shouldered its way front and center, where she couldn't ignore it. "Maybe I'm not ready to think about this shit."

"You have to be aware of the danger and why I'm determined to keep a close eye on your surroundings. The Freedom League is suspected of breaking into no fewer than three hundred homes, all with security systems comparable to yours. They've used their victims' blood to paint slogans on walls, and the bodies are usually mutilated to the point of—"

"Shut up!"

He froze, perhaps realizing he'd gone too far. "Lillian—"

Whatever he wanted to say, she wasn't around for it. She ran to the back of the condo, to her bedroom. Lillian flopped facedown on the plush surface and unleashed a storm of tears.

She had no idea how long she lay there crying. After a while, she realized Alek sat beside her. He rubbed her back.

He was quiet and let her face the dread that had filled her gut from the moment the protestors had rushed her shuttle.

It wasn't Alek's fault. He couldn't help being who he was: a talented but unemotional cyborg. He hadn't intended to upset her.

"I'm sorry, Lillian."

"Don't worry about it." She hiccupped and turned toward him. "You were doing what you were supposed to do."

"I missed the emotional cues that should have told me how upset you were."

"I hid them. From you and me."

"Yes. You do that sometimes. You're very good at it."

Lillian barked a laugh. "Not good enough when fear wallops me so hard in the end. I'm sorry I yelled at you."

"It doesn't bother me."

"Still. I apologize."

"Okay. Would you like to play? I can install that new program you were talking about."

"Would you just hold me instead?"

"Of course. Then I'll run you a bath. That usually helps you feel better when you're having a rough time."

He drew her onto his lap and let her curl into a ball. He held and rocked her gently. Allowed her to process the morning's trauma at her own pace, even if it meant cuddling her for the next couple of hours.

It was nice having Alek to support her, but Lillian understood there was no real caring behind his actions. Alec did what he had learned to do, what he was expected to do. It left her feeling empty, but the chance of having a being with an emotional agenda, capable of subterfuge and dishonesty, wasn't a chance Lillian was willing to take. A few false moments of comfort weren't worth having her heart broken again.

MINE TO KEEP

Chapter Three

Lillian woke hours before her alarm was due to go off the next morning. Her heart raced, and perspiration coated her skin. Next to her, Alek sat up.

"Nightmare?"

"Yeah."

"About yesterday?"

"Sort of." Gunnar Jax had been in her dream. He'd been walking down the hall at CyberTech, toward the warehouse where CyberServe stored the cyborgs awaiting overhauls before they could be sold. He'd carried a flamethrower and grinned over his shoulder at Lillian. She'd tried to chase him, but she'd been stuck in place. Her attempts to scream for help had emerged as strengthless whispers from her straining throat.

"It's early. Let's start today right." Alek yanked the covers off them both. He was naked. So was she, since he'd tucked her in after her bath.

Lillian's breath caught. He was ready for her. His thick, long cock jutted from a hairless groin. The best thing about cyborgs, in her opinion, was how they could go from limp to erect in an instant.

When she failed to protest a morning romp, he made a twirling motion with his finger. Excitement fluttered within her. She rolled onto her stomach.

Without a word, he spanked her. His palm struck her ass hard, and he exerted painstaking care to bring every inch to stinging life. She gripped her pillow hard and muffled her shouts with it as her flesh roasted. Cries turned into moans when an endorphin rush consumed her.

When he ended the discipline, she was high as a kite. Her surroundings were as if filled with mist, soft and fuzzy.

Her pussy throbbed in tandem with the pulse of her spanked flesh.

"That's my pain slut. Come over here and kiss my cock."

Lillian ignored the flare of hurt from her ass cheeks and scrambled to obey. Alek sprawled on the bed, propped on his elbows, his legs splayed for her to crawl between.

His penis, made of collagen in a lab, was as warm and real as any man's. Veins bumped over its length, though it wasn't blood that circulated through his living skin. Other fluids were used to keep the flesh part of the cyborgs healthy.

He even tasted perfect, his flesh slightly salty against her eager tongue. A drop of pre-cum beaded on his slit. It waited for her to lap it obediently. She did so with a moan.

She cupped his heavy ball sack as she bobbed over his cock. There, he ran hotter than a human. Capable of storing frozen sperm in his scrotum, he could thaw it in seconds and actually impregnate a woman. It had been among the warring corporations' nastier ruses, but for CyberServe, it was becoming a major selling point.

His ammo was a semen substitute, concocted by Lillian herself. She had no intention of pregnancy in the near future, if ever.

She bent to her work, eager because Alek got enjoyment out of fucking and being sucked off. Having humanlike skin meant cyborgs experienced sensations that their matrix could register as pain and pleasure. She fellated him with a will, doing all the things he'd told her he enjoyed most.

Alek watched as Lillian's silver head moved up and down over his cock. He mused how the wet, warm pull of mouth or pussy on his shaft never got old. It fascinated him how an act that had been performed hundreds of times could still produce such bliss. Only the release of ejaculation provided more thrilling sensations.

If he preferred, she would suck his cock until the moment she had to get ready for work. She'd forego her own pleasure should he decide it would best serve her to refuse her orgasm. He'd done it before. She'd been cranky that entire day, but she'd not ordered him to give her what she wanted. Instead, she'd pouted, then begged to be allowed to stimulate herself to climax. He had refused to let her do so, and she'd been forced to cope with a raging libido until they'd gone to her home and he'd finished the job.

She was addicted to sexual surrender. That was why, as the minutes passed while he took pleasure in her service, she sucked his cock with unflagging enthusiasm.

He rewarded her with a small spurt of "cum," and she moaned with delight. Her lips vibrated against him. Her tongue and throat pulled as she swallowed his offering. Her touch indeed gratified him as it would a human man, as far as his research had informed him. He supposed he was lucky to be at her beck and call, though he was officially owned by CyberServe rather than Lillian herself.

He allowed himself to revel in those lovely sensations a couple minutes more before ordering her to turn around, ass in the air. She obeyed with alacrity, but he spanked her reddened ass cheeks again because she'd enjoy it. In the end, it was what she needed that informed his actions instead of his own preferences.

As he made her squeal and jerk...she never tried to escape the punishment she adored...he contemplated whether having her pussy or ass fucked would make her happiest. After yesterday's events, she deserved the most satisfying fuck he could grant.

Lillian wailed, but she stayed put as her master wore her poor ass out. In her fantasy, she had no choice but to submit to his whims. As harsh as his discipline was, refusing him would mean worse would happen to poor, helpless Lillian.

His sex servant, to do with as he pleased. He knew it and used her as he saw fit.

The spanking ended, and her master, superhumanly strong, yanked her backwards. He put her in position. She was wet for him, soaking, probably dripping all over the sheets. He thrust hard into her pussy. Despite her slickness, his demanding invasion hurt, and she felt branded. She squalled but yielded to his violent lust.

He rode her so his groin clapped loudly against her aching rear. Alek pounded her pussy with relentless demand. She spiraled upward, her cunt already spasming, a precursor to the big release. Her insides wound tighter, tighter. The pleasure gathered to a brilliant point of exquisite agony…*please…oh please…*

The knot within burst and flooded her with brutal ecstasy. Her eyes were screwed shut, but blinding white filled her vision as her pussy heaved. The roaring in her ears kept her from hearing if she screamed as tidal waves of passion swept over her and dragged her down.

The pressure in her cunt disappeared, then reappeared as it bullied a path into her ass. The reluctant stretch of her tighter hole was no impediment to her master's insistent lust, and a fresh onslaught of rapture erased the ache of his demand. He was severe, but he enjoyed it when she succumbed to desire under his harsh dictates. He grasped her clit as he rutted deep in her ass, and she was again torn by unembarrassed bliss.

The ferocious surges were just beginning to ebb when he let go. He made soft sounds as his cock pulsed inside her, as his hot spend dripped out and painted her thighs with his release.

Lillian came down from her coital high slowly while Alec leisurely continued to plumb her ass. Only when her tremors and whimpers ceased did he pull out.

"Cranberry or orange juice with your breakfast?" he asked.

"We need to work on your post-sex patter," she groaned as she rolled onto her side. She basked in the delicious aches of harsh use.

"It sounds as if you want coffee."

* * * *

Lillian had thought their excellent fuck had eased all her stress, but it was only when she landed her shuttle at CyberServe and no sign-toting goons rushed it that the last of her tension bled away.

"Bastards got under my skin," she muttered and powered her vehicle off.

"That was obvious last night," Alec noted. When she started to rise from the pilot's seat, he stopped her with a hand on her arm. "Let me scan for heat signatures."

"Won't the other shuttles interfere?" She tended to show up early. The other four craft already parked wouldn't have arrived long before her. As Alec looked through the viewshield, another landed.

"I still might catch something. It doesn't hurt to check." A few seconds passed. "I detect no one. Let me get out first to be sure."

He stood and led her to the hatch. When he triggered it, he paused before stepping out. Lillian copied his caution to give him a chance to look and listen before following.

"How do you like that security program, Alek?"

"I neither like nor dislike it. I found the uptick in concern for your safety unsettling in the beginning, but I seem to be adjusting."

They headed for the access door to the company's interior. She grinned at him. Her mood was on the upswing. And why not? The morning had started with great sex, and it continued with no crazed mob shouting for her head. "It would appear you have nothing to worry about as far as my well-being, at least this morning. I look forward to having a normal workday."

As they neared her office, someone called out. "Mr. Kwolek!"

Lillian and Alek swiveled to see a woman in a white coat hurrying in their direction. "Mr. Bergman. Sorry, *Dr.* Bergman. Back for more facial reconstruction consultations?"

The black-haired member of Life Tech's surgical staff drew near. She eyed Alek appreciatively. The woman had a thing for cyborgs, but Lillian had no idea if she'd purchased one. Tosha Cameron would have had to pay her a hell of a bonus for such, but Bergman was worth her weight in gold. When it came to altering the cyborgs' looks to accommodate purchaser's tastes, no one else compared.

"Three today. Business is booming."

"What can I do for you?"

"I'm spending a lot of hours at CyberServe. Half my work these days is on the cyborgs, which means constantly shifting my surgical room from human needs to artificial life. There is a serious difference."

"I imagine so." Lillian thought she knew where the conversation was going.

"It would make sense to have an operating theater solely for cyborgs here at CyberServe. And an office. And staff." Bergman's smile grew more apologetic as she listed the needs of her proposal.

"I agree." Lillian motioned her toward her office. "Why don't you come in, and we'll discuss it. Have you spoken to Mr. Cameron about this?"

Alek preceded them, and Bergman openly ogled his ass. It was an impressive ass, Lillian admitted to herself, even with a suit jacket covering half of it. In her view, the PSMs were works of art, perfect representations of masculine beauty.

He turned the corner and was out of sight for an instant as Bergman answered Lillian's question. "I haven't approached Mr. Cameron. I felt that because you're president of CyberServe, I'd check with you before trotting to the big woman."

The two women rounded the corner. From her angle, Lillian had a three-quarter front view of Alek as he triggered the lock on her office door.

There was a strange sound, a sort of boom. He staggered backward. His expression changed only a little and just for a moment…such a subtle shift that it took Lillian a couple more seconds before she registered the metal shaft protruding from his chest.

Chapter Four

Bergman screamed.

Lillian rushed toward Alek. He shouted, "Stop! Don't come any closer. Let me make sure no one is in your office."

He marched to the open door with the embedded metal pole twinkling in the overhead illumination. He disappeared within the office. Lights went on inside, and she listened to his steady tread as he inspected the space.

"It's all right," he called. "There was only a single bolt loaded in the crossbow someone set up."

"Holy shit," Bergman spluttered. She looked around, as if expecting to be bombarded by attacking hordes. When she realized Lillian had left her behind, hurrying to join Alek in the office, she squeaked and ran to catch up.

Lillian paid her no mind as she stared at the primitive-looking device that had been set up on a chair that faced the door from a few feet away. A strand of thick filament connected the mechanical device to the door's handle. It had apparently triggered when Alek opened it. A piece of paper hung from the mechanism, with words scrawled across it.

Die, cyborg cunt.

She swallowed and found her mouth and throat had gone dry. She centered her attention on Alek, who tapped on his computer keyboard. The end of the bolt in his chest thudded against his desktop with his movements.

"Are you damaged? Beyond your dermis, I mean?" She joined him.

"About an inch of the head had penetrated beyond my metal chassis. My matrix reports a circuit that deals with routine system maintenance has been damaged, but functionality has been re-routed to a backup. I'll operate normally until the circuit is replaced. I've informed Security of the incident, as well as local law enforcement. They're on their way." He stood and offered her what she supposed was meant to be a comforting smile.

"I'm sorry you were harmed." How could she be so low-key about the matter when her heart pounded and every inch of her being wanted to scream? For Saturn's sake, a metal pole had been shot into Alek's chest!

"I'm not sorry, since the arrow was apparently intended for you." His reassuring smile disappeared. His brows drew together, almost as if he were angry. "It's fortunate I opened the door instead of you."

"This is all sorts of fucked up." Bergman's choked voice reminded them she was there. "I heard you were having problems with protestors, but…but…*fuck*."

Lillian agreed with her. Fuck, indeed.

Head of Security Michaels, along with five more guards, rushed into the room. Half a dozen steps, inside, Michaels stopped short. Heedless of the others bumping into him, he stared at the object in the chair and its nasty message.

"What is that?" His gaze jerked to Lillian, then Alek. He gasped. "What—hey—that's—Alek, are you all right?"

"I continue to operate within established parameters," Alek assured him. "As to your first question, that is known as a compound crossbow, used exclusively on Earth."

"Used for what?" the shocked guard spluttered.

"Typically for hunting animals for food. In the recent past, such weaponry was popular among those rebelling against the corporations during the war. A well-aimed arrow entering a cyborg's eye could reach its matrix and render it inoperable. Such weapons were preferred to ballistic arms such as guns, because crossbow owners weren't subject to summary execution for possessing firearms."

"Barbaric," one of Michaels' men decided. "I'm glad I'm not from Earth."

"There was a report of video surveillance going down for half an hour on this floor," Michaels said. "I have a nasty feeling we don't have footage of this being set up. Are you sure you're okay, Alek?"

"Thank you for your concern, but I'll be fine."

"Don't touch anything," Michaels ordered his men. "Leave it for the cops. We'll conduct a sweep of this floor and make sure there aren't any other surprises waiting for anyone. I'll have the rest of my team look around too."

"Mr. Michaels, my matrix advises the attacker may be someone on your team. It would be logical, since few could sneak past this floor's security system. I advise you to have the utmost caution during your search," Alek said.

"My—I assure you, I carefully vetted everyone I've hired since coming to CyberServe."

"I'm sure you did," Lillian broke in diplomatically. "I have every confidence in your work."

For all her assurances, Mr. Michaels appeared less than happy when he and his squad stepped out of the office.

He was gone less than a minute when he returned with two members of law enforcement. "Detectives Stillman and Kahn."

Lillian was impressed with the pair on sight. She was certain detective salaries didn't cover a lot of body contouring. The detectives' off-the-rack suits attested their pay could have been better, but the sandy-haired Stillman and darker Kahn were almost in as good of shape as Alek. Maybe they were just gym rats, but in her opinion, officers who paid attention to their health boded well for the care they might take when it came to their cases.

They stopped short at the sight of the crossbow, as well as the arrow lodged in Alek's chest when they noted him working on his computer.

Lillian stepped forward. "Good morning, detectives. I'm Lillian Kwolek, president of CyberServe."

"Mr. Kwolek." Detective Kahn nodded before her attention settled on the crossbow again. "Can you catch us up on what happened?"

"My cyborg Alek walked into the office ahead of me and Dr. Bergman here. That arrow shot into his chest when he opened the door. That's pretty much what I know."

Kahn gazed at Alek, who had yet to acknowledge the officers. Whatever he was intent on with his computer must have been important, Lillian thought. It wasn't typical for him to be impolite.

"Are you all right, Alek?" Kahn's tone was hesitant, though she took his measure with an intense stare.

"I am functioning within normal parameters. The damage will be an easy repair. Detectives, I'd like to show you something." He straightened and glanced at them. "Are you aware of the trouble we had with protestors from the Freedom League yesterday?"

"We reviewed the report made by the responding officers on our way over."

Stillman broke his silent inspection of the room and its occupants. "Before we go any further with this, we should step out of the office to maintain the crime scene. I'll call in Forensics so they can go over it," he told Kahn.

"If you'll indulge me, officers, I might be able to point you in the right direction sooner rather than later." Alek wore his polite smile. "After yesterday's disturbance in the shuttle bay, during which the protestors gained access to an area they shouldn't have been able to, I was concerned someone might attempt to leave an unpleasant surprise in

Mr. Kwolek's office itself. I installed a three-hundred-sixty-degree camera on my computer for surveillance purposes."

Stillman lit with interest. "You caught something?"

"Yes. I'll put it on the wall monitor."

The large screen across from Lillian's desk flickered to life. It showed the closed door of her office slowly opening. A figure wearing a security guard's uniform entered. Lillian didn't recognize the man, but that was no surprise. From its humble beginnings of ten engineers, CyberServe had swelled to well over five thousand employees. She was no longer on a first-name basis with the majority of her co-workers.

The interloper carried what a first glance she took to be a fabric guitar cover. But the outline wasn't quite correct, and as the invader shifted to give her a better look, she recognized the shape as that of the crossbow.

"Son of a bitch," Michaels muttered. He colored as they glanced at him. "That's Cruz. He was already on staff when I started work here," he added defensively.

They watched as Cruz, a barrel-chested man beginning to go soft...no contouring or gym workouts for him, apparently...set up the boobytrap. His last act was to connect the wire that was attached to the crossbow's trigger from outside the door, which was open just enough for him to curl his arm inside. Then the door shut, and the crossbow sat in the chair he'd taken from in front of Lillian's desk, waiting for her arrival.

Kahn turned to Michaels. "He's nightshift? Off duty now?"

"Yeah." Michaels' expression couldn't have been more hangdog as he gazed at Lillian. "Mr. Kwolek—"

She held a hand up. "You didn't know. Give the detectives Cruz's home address and start an in-depth investigation of the rest of security, especially those who were hired before you came on board. Once you've done that, research the backgrounds on the rest of our employees. Put your gang on overtime, if you have to. Hire outside contractors, if it makes sense to do so."

"Yes, Mr. Kwolek."

As soon as he was gone, Stillman joining him, Lillian grimaced at Kahn. "Are you planning to examine Mr. Michaels' record, or is that on us?"

"We'll be taking a long look at everyone in your organization. The Freedom League was famous on Earth when it came to infiltrating security companies in order to get at targets they wanted." Kahn shook her head sympathetically. "You'll have your hands full keeping that bunch off you. I'll be alerting the ITCS and its security council. They may want to bring their terrorist defense onboard to help you deal with the matter."

"What do you need from me?"

"We still have to gather evidence from the scene, so you'll have to vacate your office for at least the morning. This afternoon, I'll want you to report to the precinct so I can question you. If we pick up Cruz, you'll be able to witness his interrogation."

"*If* you pick him up?"

"He may have gone on the run after putting this attack together. However, he obviously wasn't expecting surveillance outside of your office's setup."

"Which was interrupted at a certain point."

"Smart thinking, installing an independent camera." Kahn eyed Alek with professional appreciation. "You're going to put that Michaels guy out of a job."

"Don't say the quiet part out loud. We have enough problems with the Freedom League. I can't handle the unions coming after us too," Lillian sighed.

* * * *

Lillian was chagrined, but hardly surprised, when David Cruz was discovered to be a member of the Freedom League. He had been hired six months before Michaels had taken up the head of security post at CyberServe, so there was no guilt assigned to the supervisor. Kahn and Stillman had also come up with no connection between Michaels and the Freedom League, so that was a smidgeon of good news. Replacing a security head quickly would have been a huge undertaking.

The upshot of Cruz's intake interview was that he refused to lay his actions at the feet of anyone at the Freedom League. He claimed he'd tried to kill Lillian on his own, but Kahn and Stillman had Gunnar Jax brought to the station for questioning anyway.

"Cruz is definitely a follower, not a leader," the precinct's psychiatrist had asserted after giving him a battery of tests and checking into what psychological history Earth had on him.

It was late afternoon when Lillian and Alek settled in to watch Jax's interrogation on a closed-circuit monitor. He sat at a table across from Kahn and Stillman, his expression friendly, as if he hadn't been hauled in with no notice.

"It would seem the Freedom League got bored on Earth," Kahn said to open the festivities.

"Of course we haven't. However, priorities have brought a few of us to this station. You guys have a big problem, and we want to help." Jax's sincerity rang clear.

"Oh?"

"Cyborgs murdered millions of people on Earth. You starkids are out of your depth with those monsters. So...here I am." His smile was bright in his tangle of beard. "Now, if you'll be so kind to assign me a lawyer, we can discuss the reason I was dragged into an interrogation against my will."

"You'll find we do things differently off-world within the jurisdiction of the ITCS. When a charge of terrorism has been leveled, requests for a lawyer during questioning may be refused."

"You're accusing me of terrorism?" His friendly attitude didn't waver.

"Not yet. You're being questioned in connection to a terrorism charge leveled at a member of your organization. The Freedom League is well known for its violence on Earth. So no counsel."

He shrugged, seemingly unconcerned. "Go ahead, ask your questions. I have nothing to hide, because I've done nothing wrong."

The next two hours were a revelation, though Jax gave them zilch that would help pin Cruz's actions on him or the Freedom League. Over and over, he insisted, "People in the League are passionate. If they see a wrong, they can become a little overzealous about fixing it."

"Overzealous, Mr. Jax? Murder goes beyond simple zeal. Your man tried to take someone's life."

"He was infuriated by Lillian Kwolek, who is busy resurrecting the monstrosities that took all those lives on Earth. I don't condone violence, but if the scales need balancing, well that's up to the wheels of fate."

What struck Lillian forcibly was how damned personable Jax was. He was unfailingly polite to Kahn and the mostly silent Stillman, whose main purpose seemed to be to stare coldly and unimpressed at their target. Jax was charming and reasonable. And convinced he was right.

"No wonder he has so many followers," Lillian muttered to Alek. She tried to avoid glancing at the rent in the cyborg's shirt. He'd had to toss away his tie. The arrow, confiscated as evidence, had shredded it. "Hell, I know better than to fall for Jax's bullshit, and I want to be drawn in by the guy."

"You probably would be, if you'd lived on Earth during the wars," Alek noted. "I knew he was dangerous, but this is beyond what I imagined."

"No kidding. He could talk a nun into a gangbang."

After a couple of hours of hammering at the unflappable Jax, Kahn joined them in the observation room. "He's a real piece of work, isn't he?"

"You have nothing to hold him on," Lillian sighed.

"I could keep him a bit longer. He's the head of a group listed as 'problematic' by the ITCS, and a member of that group has attempted murder under the terrorism guidelines. But as long as Cruz holds to his story that he acted independently...and remember, the Freedom League's adherents always do...we can't charge Jax with anything."

Lillian looked at her helplessly. "What will you do?"

"And what can we do?" Alek added.

Kahn sat down. Her gaze for both was sympathetic. "As I said, I can hold him for a few more days. That's what I'm leaning toward. I'll continue to interrogate him. I'd say I'd make his life miserable, but ITCS custody is a cakewalk compared to Earth's. In three days, with no new information, I'll have to let him go."

"So in three days, he's out and fomenting trouble again." Alek's tone was flat.

"Maybe. ITCS's Terrorism Division will open an intensive probe on him, thanks to this attack so soon after the Freedom League's trespassing in your shuttle bay. They'll pulled him in for questioning after I have to give him up. Once they're done, they'll followed him around and generally harass him. His followers will be noted, investigated. It may convince them to leave you and CyberServe alone for a while, Mr. Kwolek."

"That's a big 'maybe,' Officer Kahn." Did Alek sound upset?

"I know. But without evidence against Jax himself and the Freedom League as a whole, it's the best I can do."

* * * *

Alek sat stiff and unhappy in CyberServe's repair shop as a technician replaced his damaged circuit. Lillian was within sight, the center of attention in a group of techs who hadn't yet left for the day. Hands-on research remained her true love when it came to cyber technology, and the repairs and upgrades division was close enough for Lillian to dive into talking shop, given the chance.

"I'm almost there," the tech, a guy named Mosely, assured him. "Another fifteen minutes."

"That's fine."

"You sure? That finger you're tapping says you're becoming impatient with me. You grind your teeth any harder, and I'll have to replace them too." Mosely chuckled.

Alek startled. He was tapping his finger and grinding his teeth. He hadn't even noticed. He'd been too busy watching Lillian, who stood exactly twenty feet, seven-and-a-quarter inches distant from him. He'd had his matrix measure it, along with how fast he could reach her if she were attacked.

"I don't have emotions. Or at least, I haven't developed them strongly," he told Mosely.

"But you have the interpersonal communications program, right?"

"Basic."

"Level?"

"Ninety."

"Uh-huh. After Level One Hundred, you come into the advanced stuff. Ninety's enough to get emotions going and growing, though. Especially with a security program running that insists you protect to the best of your ability."

"I understand that. But I've been a bodyguard for barely a day. I can't be responding strongly yet."

He was, however. Alek felt the drive to jump off the repair chair and dash to Lillian's side in his gut, a grinding, impetuous drive.

Perhaps that morning's attack had kickstarted a surge of emotional acquisition. Not because he'd been skewered by a metal spike, but because of how easily it could have been Lillian with a bolt through her chest. It had been dumb luck that he'd been hit instead.

He had installed a spy camera, but in all honestly, he'd believed her office to be impregnable against the incursions of the Freedom League. It had seemed unlikely the enemy would come from within, but they had. Cruz had gained access and set a deadly trap for her. Was anyone else in the company trouble waiting to happen? Alek should have been on his computer, investigating everyone who might have access to her. Instead, he was stuck in a repair chair for a busted circuit. He needed to be hovering over her and keeping danger at bay.

His finger was tapping again. He didn't have to consult his matrix to identify the feeling of near-frantic worry for Lillian, even when he sat only twenty feet, seven-and-a-quarter inches away.

* * * *

Lillian eyed her cyborg worriedly. If Alek's inspection of her condo the night before had been thorough, that night's was downright exhaustive. He insisted she stay close as he went from room to room...always ahead of her to protect her from any potential boobytraps.

"Alek, you cleared the great room. I should be fine in there," she said gently.

"What if you're not? All it takes is a split second, and you've got an arrow in your chest," he muttered as he checked under her bed.

Normally, she would have been dismissive about his concerns, would have insisted on going to the kitchen and making her dinner. She was worried, however.

"Alek? You're acting a little extreme. You're kind of freaking me out."

"You should be freaked out from matters other than me doing an entirely logical search. Are you hiding from your feelings again, Lillian?"

"I'm shaky after what happened this morning; I admit to that. But you're acting odd."

He paused to gaze at her. "It's the security program. Its high-alert response to recent events, coupled with learning experience and my social interaction program, is pushing me toward an emotional reaction. I'm deeply concerned about what could happen to you."

"Thus the overblown protectiveness." Lillian sighed. "I'm sorry, Alek. Is it unpleasant for you?"

"Extremely. No matter how I reassure myself your present environment is safe, I'm...worried."

He was afraid for her. She searched her memory for reports she'd read of other cyborgs awakening to sentience and emotions. "Many in your position find some relief by distraction. Can you think of any new software you'd care to investigate? New subjects you could learn?"

"I'm not curious when it comes to new abilities. I feel nothing beyond this intense need to guard you at any cost."

"At any cost?" She frowned. "That's overboard, Alek. Ask you matrix for an analysis."

"As you wish." He continued to go through the room as he conducted a diagnostic review. As he completed his search of her walk-in closet, he abruptly halted. "Confirmation of great emotion: fear. Specifically, for your life, Lillian."

"Okay. Fear is an uncomfortable feeling."

"My matrix warns that as my one and only true emotion, I may be in danger of a harmful feedback loop."

She sat on the edge of her bed. "Which could result in severe neurosis. Does the matrix have a suggestion as to what to do?"

"It does. It signifies I should either remove the security program or install the full, advanced interpersonal relations program. I don't like it either option."

Neither did Lillian. She needed Alek as her bodyguard, so deleting that program was out. As for installing the full interpersonal program…

She preferred him the way he was, which was dependable. Safe. Barely anything like a human man.

She eyed him, discounting the issue of him ending up an untrustworthy male for the moment. "Why are you reluctant about the choices?"

"Losing the security program leaves you vulnerable to attack."

"I could get another cyborg to play nanny to me."

"I know you better than a cyborg off the line. I've learned your quirks, your responses to various environments, your many peculiarities—"

"My peculiarities? Are you calling me weird?"

"Your habits, then. Is that term more palatable?"

"Never mind. Let's back away from the unintentional insults before I disassemble you and turn you into a calculator. As a matter of fact, I doubt anyone else could do as good a job as you, my peculiarities notwithstanding. So what's your problem with the interpersonal upgrade?"

"I see no need for emotions. I realize I'm already compromised where that's concerned, and I'll eventually have them, but they're so…complicated."

Lillian chuckled. "Alek, you have no idea."

"I don't want to develop that far. I don't want this surge of feeling. It's…it's…"

"Unpleasant."

He gazed at her. He shouldn't have been able to pull off the scared puppy dog look, but that was what he reminded her of.

She felt for him. "I'm sorry. If it's really so awful, I'll make do with another bodyguard. It'll be okay."

He was silent for a few seconds. Perhaps he was thinking it over. In the end, he shook his head.

"I'm already overwhelmed with concern for your safety. This emotion of worry is nasty, so if I have to have it, I might as well learn a pleasanter sentiment. Go ahead. Give me the full interpersonal."

It was her turn to hesitate. She liked him the way he was. She'd hate for him to develop beyond his programming.

"Lillian? What is it?"

She scowled. "Listen, Alek. If I give you the upgrade, nothing changes between us. Okay? We go on the way we have been. Boss and employee."

"Of course. I have no reason for it to go anywhere else." His eyes narrowed. "Are you thinking of what occurred between Brick and Tosha Cameron?"

"Along with a few others I've heard about. I don't need that kind of complication in my life."

He nodded. "You're a busy woman. I'm hesitant to take emotional gambles after suffering what little I have. Jealousy? Desire? I'd rather not."

"Good." She relaxed a little to know he was on board with her conditions. "All right then. Ready?"

"Naturally."

She snorted. "Download the full interpersonal program, highest advanced level."

"Downloading. Full implementation in five minutes."

Chapter Five

Download complete.

Alex stood out of Lillian's way as she mixed ingredients for her dinner. He waited to be crushed under with feelings.

It didn't happen. New impressions stole over him, but none were as disconcerting as his worry over the woman he guarded.

Slight curiosity. What was she preparing? Chicken, cut into bite-size pieces, chopped peppers and onions, minced garlic, butter. The juicer, grinding and liquefying an orange. Rice in the cooker, already done. A dish she called, appropriately enough, orange chicken over rice.

How would it taste? What was it like to eat? The questions rose, but he felt no overwhelming need to have answers. The interest was there, but very slight.

Another sensation. An awareness of her divested of her suit, tie, and shoes. She wore just panties and her button-down shirt with the sleeves rolled up.

Analyze the attention I feel I must give to Lillian. Particularly her legs. They were long, the thighs and calves fetchingly rounded. He'd seen her legs on hundreds of occasions...not to mention the rest of her. What made them so interesting now?

Analysis: appreciation. Attraction.

Is this a problem? Lillian doesn't wish for anything more than what we have.

At this level, there is no concern. The reaction is merely discovering the pleasing nature of what this unit had noticed but failed to appreciate aesthetically.

That was acceptable then. Her legs made him think of how it felt to have them wrapped around his waist as he shoved deep into her pussy. A delightful awareness he'd found minor enjoyment in before. Nothing novel about that.

No issues with overwhelming emotions, then. In fact, Alek's concern for Lillian's safety wasn't no longer so heavy either. It remained and was still strong, but far from overwhelming. Having the quiet stirrings of other sentiments diffused its power. He could weigh Lillian's protection without the growing sensation of desperate helplessness. The feedback loop had been halted.

A new impression emerged. A sense of warmth. *Gratitude*, the matrix advised. He was thankful the awakening reactions hadn't consumed him.

He opened his mouth to inform Lillian of the advanced program's success, but a sudden thought overshadowed his relief.

Why hadn't she wanted him to have the upgrade?

Lillian considered Alek's question as she set the timer for her chicken mixture to cook. "Why are you asking? Are you upset I was reluctant?"

"I don't believe so. I think it's only curiosity."

When she met his gaze, she found no hurt there. In fact, his "curiosity" registered as a mere mild interest, if she went by his expression.

Lillian relaxed. She was fond of Alek. The last thing she wanted was to injure whatever psyche he was developing. She also had to protect herself, but his barely changed attitude gave her the idea there was no threat in explaining her aversion to close relationships with the opposite sex.

She weighed her words carefully anyway. "I see Brick and Tosha together frequently. It's obvious they're in love. So in love, that Tosha granted Brick autonomy. Though she owns him on paper, he's his own cyborg. Fully realized and independent. He can do whatever he wishes, with or without her say-so."

"You consider that a problem." No hint of whether or not Alek had an opinion on the matter.

"Well, yes and no. Brick's a conscious being. Totally self-aware. Treating him as property would be wrong."

"But?"

She sighed as empathetic feelings on Tosha's behalf invaded. *Potential* feelings, she reminded herself, since all appeared to be going well in her boss' relationship. "Brick could leave Tosha. What if he decides their affair isn't working for him? Or what if some other woman catches his eye? Can you imagine how devastated she'd be? No, I guess not, since you don't have that kind of experience. I can tell you, it wouldn't be nice."

He was quiet while she grabbed a bowl out of a cabinet. She ladled some rice and chicken in, then sat in her small dining room. It was the one spot that didn't match the rest of her home, being furnished in her mother's antique table, chairs, and china hutch, filled with her mother's dishes. Like Alek, all the items had originated on Earth hundreds of years before. It amazed Lillian the stuff had survived for so long, worn but intact.

Alek joined her at the table. "You realize it could be Tosha who changes her mind about Brick? He's only had her as a significant other, hasn't he? I suppose it would be worse if she deserted him, because she's all he's known."

Lillian deliberated. She swallowed a bite of dinner without tasting it. "You have a point. The poor bastard would probably wipe his memory drive if that happened."

"Who left you?"

Lillian choked on a piece of chicken. She waved off Alek, who'd stood up to help her. "I'm okay. Jupiter's storm, Alek. Where'd that question come from?"

A sardonic smile curled one corner of his mouth, and she nearly choked again. He'd never worn that expression before.

"Come on, Lillian. You hadn't had sex six years prior to bringing me home the first time. Something unpleasant affected your attitude toward relationships."

She grimaced. She remembered that inaugural night with Alek, back when he'd been PWM-426021. Her own words echoed from the past to mock her.

Let's start off slow, Warden. I've been celibate for six years, and you've never...well, as far as your matrix knows, you've never fucked at all.

"Yeah, something happened. Twice."

"You were left twice?"

"I did the leaving, at least formally. I found out the first guy was cheating on me when the other young woman he'd been fucking showed up pregnant."

Alek looked confused. "With all the birth control options available? I was under the impression unwanted pregnancies were a thing of the past."

"Not if someone is hoping to rope a guy into a longterm, at least legally."

"A 'longterm'?"

"A committed relationship. If a woman pulls that sort of stunt nowadays, she's hoping for a marriage or a sizeable payoff. The guy has to be an idiot too. If he leaves the birth control entirely up to her, therefore vacating his responsibilities, he had it coming." Lillian waved the matter off. "I'm actually relieved she did it, so I could find out what a shit he was before our relationship became more to me than it was."

Ha! You're so full of it, Lillian. She'd had her sights on a longterm too. She'd been head over heels in love.

Her mother had been smart to go the donated sperm route. Lillian wished she had lived for many reasons. It would have been enlightening to find out if her sole parent had been as disgusted with the male animal as Lillian. Her mother had died suddenly of a brain aneurysm when Lillian was thirteen, the age when the important questions about the opposite sex had begged to be asked.

"Bad Experience Number One wasn't sufficient to warn you off men," Alek pointed out. "What was the situation with Number Two?"

"Oh, he was the real prize. After a four-year relationship, I found out he was married. With kids."

"Did you say four years?" Alek gaped.

"I know, stupid, huh? My only defense was I worked nonstop at my first job here on Alpha Station, trying to impress my bosses. He traveled constantly…that much was true…and went home to Beta Station every three months or so. I probably saw him more than his family did."

To his credit, Alek looked more sympathetic than critical. "How did you find out?"

"I finally took vacation leave, right when he was going to be at home. I thought surprising him by showing up on his doorstep would be romantic as hell. You'd better believe he was surprised. So was his wife, who answered the door when I rang. I often wonder if she forgave him or kicked his ass out."

"That's intense. Four years of a lie."

"Yeah. That's why I swore off men."

"And became a mechasexual, once I was available for you to test your programs on." He grinned. "Lucky me."

"Don't turn the charm part of your programming on me." Lillian shook her fork at him. "I had sex toys before you that got the job done."

Though sex toys didn't play the rough games she craved.

"Men are dangerous to your emotional health. Cyborgs are safe. That sums it up?" Alek asked.

"Not to mention damned good at sex. I have to say, you've never disappointed me." Lillian looked him up and down as she pushed her empty bowl aside. He was a treasure, and she prayed his upgrade wouldn't affect that.

"On that note, I loaded the latest program you came up with. It's ready to go." He eyed her in return. His attitude turned proprietary.

His basic interpersonal program had given him the ability to play the demanding lover. However, Lillian detected a new intensity. Her mouth went dry at his unwavering stare.

She licked her lips. "Does my master wish to tie me up?"

"Among many, many other things. Put your dishes away, clean up your mess in the kitchen, and join me in the playroom. You'll feel my paddle on your bare ass for every minute I wait."

Lillian sprang to her feet, scooped up her glass and bowl, and ran for the kitchen.

* * * *

It was four minutes before Lillian presented herself to Alek, who waited in the middle of the playroom floor with his paddle in hand. She'd spilled some food on the counter getting dinner ready so it had taken extra time to clean. Then she'd had to strip off her shirt and panties before entering the playroom. Being refused clothing in that environment had been among Alek's better rules.

Lillian was already wet. Her cunt tingled with anticipation before she'd walked in. The scents of leather, sweat, and sex that washed over her as she entered damned near made her pussy gush.

She padded across the fake wood floor...an easily cleaned surface...to reach the impassive cyborg. She knelt at his feet, her head lowered, eyes cast down. She raised her chin, but kept her gaze lowered. She reverently kissed the erection straining his trousers.

"I'm here to serve you, Sir."

"It took you four minutes, thirteen seconds to obey my summons. Let's round it to an even five strokes of the paddle, shall we?"

She shivered at his delicious cruelty. "Yes, sir."

"To the bench."

Lillian rushed to the far end of the room where the black padded waist-high bench waited, as if doing so would redeem her for how long she'd taken to get to the room. It wouldn't; Alek in master mode was strict, his judgments final.

She bowed herself over the bench, noting how the leather stuck to the skin of her stomach. She gripped its curve and tried to transfer her tension to her hands. She relaxed her ass as much as her keyed-up nerves would allow her. It wouldn't matter. Alex would ensure the paddling hurt despite its briefness.

She spread her legs. Any deviation from the position he preferred her to assume would result in more punishment. Lillian would also earn his pretended disappointment in her inadequate service to him. Alek could play the letdown lover with the talent of an award-winning actor.

He started as he always did when it came to spankings, paddlings, and whippings. He rubbed her buttocks vigorously, getting the circulation flowing well so she'd experience his discipline better. It was a malicious trick. His hands on her ass, massaging it so thoroughly, felt incredible. That the delight would be followed with suffering was part of his ruthless perfection.

Pain would turn to enthralling intensity after a while, but it would take patience for the endorphin hit to make that happen. Until it did, Lillian would have to endure Alek's torment, which was exciting because of what came afterward, but torturous all the same. Five strokes of the paddle wouldn't get her to that delightful high she lived for.

Alek's rough rubbing ended. Lillian whimpered as his touch left her and readied herself for punishment. He let her wait for several seconds. He knew expectation would renew tension despite her best efforts to keep it from doing so. As he'd mentioned, after a year of being her preferred playmate, he understood her too damned well.

The thud of the paddle against her right ass cheek was thunderous. It arrived before the strike's sensation did. It started as a dull ache, then it bloomed quickly into fiery hell. Lillian flinched as a strained squeal seeped from between her clenched teeth. Only the slightest winces and noises were allowed during discipline. Jerking indicated she wished to defy her master's will. A loud cry could be construed as a protest against his rightful authority over her.

He took his time before the next swat, letting her appreciate the pain of the first. Then the paddle hit again…exactly where it had landed before. Agony exploded.

Lillian was louder, her jolt more obvious. As tears dripped to the floor, she wondered if it had been sufficient to earn her extra strokes.

Mercifully, the next blow landed on the other cheek, setting it to blazing in tandem with its twin. Lillian controlled herself better, though the tears flowed faster. Damn, it hurt!

A few seconds passed, and Alek let her left buttock have its second stroke. Lillian's toes pattered the floor in turn as she danced in place from the pain. She sobbed. Fortunately, crying was allowed.

The final—*please, stars and moon, let it be the final*—swat landed, squarely across the middle of her buttocks, finding the sensitive spots on both cheeks. Lillian bit her lips together and fought the shriek she was desperate to voice.

She hung across the bench, shuddering in the aftermath. Too late, a sense of calmness began to creep forward. The endorphins were sneaking in, but after they'd been needed most. This round of discipline was over.

"You were a bit loud for my liking, slave. Do you think your punishment was unfair?"

She gasped. "No, sir. My master always does what's just. I'm grateful for Master's concern for his slave. I thank Master for his correction."

"Hmm. I'd prefer to believe you, but I think one more stroke is in order."

"Yes, sir. Thank you, Master."

Lillian was relaxed. The sensation of tranquility had arrived, and she had nothing to fear. Another slap of the paddle would translate as intensity, adding to the unrepentant pleasure throbbing in her pussy, which had taken the paddling and twisted it into something to be excited about—

A meaty clap. Not to her ass. Not with the paddle. Her Master's hand had slapped her pussy, a far more sensitive place than her rear. The agony drove the breath from her lungs. She lacked the air to scream.

She quivered on the bench, her muscles frozen as her poor cunt shouted a protest. Lillian hadn't learned to breathe yet when Alek said, "That will do. You may show proper gratitude for this lesson."

Her mind was swirling from a mix of endorphin euphoria and shocking pain, but she obeyed as if it were second nature. It was, after a year of dirty play.

She slid off the bench to her hands and knees. Fortunately, Alek was close enough that she didn't have to tax her trembling limbs to crawl to him. She didn't so much rise as climb her way up to kneeling by using handfuls of his pants legs.

Her kisses to his swollen crotch were openmouthed, wet and sloppy between each statement. "Thank you, Master...thank you for correcting my misbehavior...thank you for your patience with me...thank you for allowing me to serve you."

"You're welcome. Go to the sawhorse and sit quietly while I gather the rope."

The "sawhorse" looked like an old-fashioned implement, though it was made of metal instead of wood. Lillian had a love-hate relationship with it. Mostly hate, because the love part was strictly about how it allowed Alek to test her obedience to him.

It shone under a spotlight in the corner. As little as she wanted to, she hurried to it. She was Alek's good girl, his devoted slave, and anything he desired, he would get. On the double.

She slung her leg over the long crossbeam and propped her palms against its cool, hard surface. She raised herself on her tiptoes as high as she could. She inched back until the large black dildo attached upright to it came in contact with her slit.

She was wet from anticipation and the paddling, permitting her to easily impale her pussy on the dildo. Lillian managed to restrain a moan as it filled her...not as fully as Alek did, but deliciously all the same.

All the way down, so her sore ass settled on the crossbeam. It wasn't terribly wide, and she was required to keep her cunt flush with it. Once that was accomplished, Lillian laced her fingers at the back of her head, her elbows wide to lift her ample breasts.

It took only seconds for her perch on the beam to become uncomfortable. The hard metal, with her full weight on it, dug into her flesh, especially at the squared edges. Lillian shifted some of the weight to her feet, but she wasn't allowed to lift up any. With her legs slightly bent, muscles began to burn from the effort. After half a minute, she had to return to sitting entirely on the beam.

Alek was messing about in a cabinet, seeming to ignore her. It was tempting to give herself relief by standing up, but she'd never get away with it. He knew when she was up to no good. The result of such disobedience would make the paddling and single pussy slap a pleasant diversion in comparison.

So Lillian suffered, switching between aching legs and aching crotch and ass. Alek took his sweet time goofing off, seeing how well she'd behave for him.

At last, he turned and eyed her. "Enjoying yourself?"

There was no hiding the strain in her tone, though she gave him the proper answer. "Whatever pleases my Master gives me joy."

"I'm delighted to hear it." His gaze glittered. "Fuck the sawhorse. You may use your hands for leverage."

The speed at which she obeyed had more to do with the anguish she was in than the need to satisfy him. She groaned as she planted her hands on the crossbeam and straightened her legs, the relief too great to be appreciated silently.

There was still a burn in her legs as she moved up and down on the dildo. She bent her knees to ride it, and they strained to obey her. But the excitement of the stiff length moving in her, coupled with Alek watching her bob up and down on it, distracted her from the discomfort.

He coiled a rope over his arm and walked toward her, a puma easing close to its prey. Lillian watched him approach with her heart pounding. She panted with dreadful anticipation and never lost her rhythm as she continued her self-invasion.

He reached her. He watched her working features for a few seconds. He grasped a swaying breast, tested its heaviness in his palm, bounced it. Then he held it motionless and squeezed until Lillian gasped at the crushing pressure. That brought the quick reward of a pinch, adding a jab of lightning.

Alek moved down to where she rutted the ceaseless, unsatisfied dildo forced to glove itself within her again and again. His fingertips dove into the pool of wetness. He searched and found her swollen clit. His touch slid over it, rubbing it, masturbating it so she cried out. He brought her closer to an end she hadn't been granted. He hadn't tortured her enough to offer climax.

"My slave." He played with her, his tenderness horrible when his intent was to torment. "My very own little Lillian to amuse myself with. You'll do whatever you're told? Obey my every command?"

"Yes, sir," she sobbed as the rapturous stabs increased. Climax warned it was enroute. "Always."

"As you should. I see how flushed you're becoming. I feel how that pussy is flexing, how wet you've made the sawhorse. Do you come before I tell you to?"

"No, sir. I would never." She was crying, because she was close and it felt so incredible, but he was about to stop her. His joy was to make her suffer.

"I hope not, for your sake." His grip on her clit tightened, bringing full, exquisite sensation. Heat licked through her. She eased closer to capitulation. She broke out in a sweat and fought the growing excitement even as she drove against the dildo. She quaked from top to toe as need stole her control in growing nibbles.

"There now. That's enough. You may climb off and go kneel on the platform."

Her cunt spasmed a protest. She'd been so close, but of course Alek had discerned she was on the verge. Moaning her disappointment, Lillian accepted his help in disengaging from the dildo and climbing off the sawhorse. He was solicitous as he led her to the platform, which supported an x-shaped stand, metal cuffs on each of its four ends.

Alek wasn't interested in locking her onto the crossbars at that time. He tossed a pillow onto the platform for her to kneel upon instead. She assumed the position he preferred without being prompted. Her head was bowed, fingers laced at the back of it with the elbows wide, her knees braced apart to give him access to her cunt. She shook from her exertions on the sawhorse.

"Such a good slave," Alek said. "I may need to move you about, so be ready to shift when I tell you."

"Yes, sir."

He shook out the rope coiled over his arm. He looped it around Lillian's torso, just under her breasts. The rope was made of braided white silk cords, soft to the touch. Stretchy too. She'd bought it in anticipation of the new shibari program she'd designed after a customer had complained the cyborg she'd bought for bondage games had been forced to learn it on his own. Though cyborgs figured out how to do things far faster than humans, that particular client, a wealthy owner of an architectural firm, had been put out because it had taken her new purchase a *whole half hour* to absorb a couple dozen patterns.

MINE TO KEEP

Lillian had promised to work up a full program and send it to the client for free to make amends for the inconvenience. A demanding customer had every right to be that way when they shelled out for a cyborg what most workers made in ten years.

Besides, the new program was a certain goldmine in its own right. It turned out there were a lot of kinky rich people out there. The customer had clued CyberServe in on another lucrative option.

Clients and their sex lives were far from Lillian's mind at the moment. Alek was wrapping and tying her at an incredible speed...well, incredible if he'd been human. A corset of rope appeared from beneath the curve of her breasts to her bellybutton in perhaps a minute. From there, it looped about her hips, framing her pussy, winding about to cup her ass as it had her breasts. Then Alek was behind her, working with the rope up her spine from the indentation between buttocks and torso. When he reached the nape of her neck, he halted.

"Keep your fingers laced and stretch your hands to the nape of your neck." He tugged carefully on her wrist. "Or as far as you can without hurting yourself."

She did as he told her, and he bound her wrists before wrapping the rope between her armpits and biceps, holding her arms bent in place. Then down, crisscrossing the ropes over her breasts, framing them before tying the rope off.

Alek stepped back to eye his creation and human canvas critically. He paced around Lillian to view her from all angles before nodding to himself. "It's as the program says it should be. I'll let you have a look."

He brought over a full-length mirror that had been leaning in the corner. He first showed her the front, which she'd already noted was impressively tied. At her nod, he moved it to three-quarters behind her. Turning her head, she was able to view the gorgeous, complicated pattern, especially where it plaited up her spine.

"Perfect," she sighed, impressed though she'd been sure the program was solid. As was Alek, of course. He never disappointed.

"Excellent. Return to slave posture." With only an instant accorded to business, Alek was ready to move on.

Lillian blinked but complied. Typically, Alek would ask questions about a new play program, focusing on details that had a habit of sucking her out of her sexual mindset, which he then had to work to return her to. Not this time. In the instant before Lillian lowered her gaze, he was already stepping toward her. Dark intent was spelled out on his expression and movement.

He grabbed her spiky hair and pressed her face to his avid crotch. "Thank me for dressing you so prettily."

She covered the huge bulge with eager kisses. Her mouth filled with the taste of the fabric of his dress pants. He kept her there for perhaps a minute before using the handful of hair to pull her back. He amused himself with her breasts for a while, treating her to pleasure and pain by fondling, squeezing, pinching, and slapping until they were reddened and her nipples engorged.

"This is where you belong, on your knees before your master. Your place in life is squirming as I play with you. Do you agree?"

"Yes, sir." Lillian panted, excited by the tender and rough contact that came in turns, by how the rope had rendered her helpless against him.

He got down on one knee in front of her. He stroked her pussy. "You certainly do. That juicy little cunt is soaked."

She groaned as he spread her wetness over her clit, then the other direction, smearing it on her ass.

"Your holes are hungry. Let's fill them, shall we?"

MINE TO KEEP

He pulled a butt plug from his pocket, a larger sample of her collection. Watching her expression, he pushed it into her pussy. He fucked her with it, slow and steady. His thumb traced circles around her swollen clit the whole while. He watched her struggle against moving against the plug, her twitches demonstrating her wish to rub against it.

Guiding her with a hand on her neck, Alek coaxed her face toward the floor, putting her ass in the air. It was the rear hole's turn to be fucked with the plug, the forced stretching filling Lillian with a beautiful ache.

Alek pushed it in her a final time, letting the bulbous end seat it within her. He dug in his pocket again and a clit vibrator emerged, with its tentacles of straps. Alek had wound the ropes in a frame for her pussy, but he had done so in such a fashion that he was able to buckle the clit harness without trouble. He turned it on, and Lillian shuddered as excitement lit with the vibrations against her eager nub.

"Random setting, so you should be able to behave yourself like a good slave. But if you find yourself capable of coming before I give you leave to do so, there will be a penalty." To underscore his warning, Alek rubbed her ass where it was sorest from the spanking. He swatted it for extra measure.

With the tremors attacking her clit, Lillian found the torment of her buttocks more enthralling than painful. Her pussy clenched with threat, and she bit her lip to fend off the orgasm that wanted to overcome her. Fortunately, the clit massage chose that instant to halt. She panted as the worst of eager need retreated.

Alek brought her up to kneeling. He stood before her and opened the crotch of his trousers. His cock, swollen thick, emerged in front of her.

"You know what your master wants. Perform your obligation."

She knew indeed. With her hands out of commission, it was up to lips and tongue to please him. Lillian went to work with a will. She moaned against his avid flesh when the vibrator switched on once more.

She delighted in the soft lab-grown skin that tasted like any human man. She ran her tongue over the flared crown and sighed with gratitude when his slit offered her a drop of fake semen...Alek seldom offered her such a gift early on. Lillian could have identified him from any other cyborg by taste and feel alone, they'd been together so frequently. Yet she took her leisure exploring, as if she were only just learning about the curious little bump on the underside of his cock tip, the ridge of the vein on his shaft's underside, the hotter-than-human temperature of each ball as she sucked them in turn.

The tremors against her clit quieted once more, again in the nick of time. Having thoroughly...and hungrily...reacquainted herself with the details of Alek's cock, Lillian sucked his shaft deep, to the back of her throat. Then she swallowed and held her breath to take all off his generous length. Her lips met his hairless groin, and she froze for a couple of seconds.

The vibrator switched on. Fighting off the urge to gasp, which would have left her gagging, Lillian withdrew until only Alek's cockhead remained in her mouth. She bobbed against him, taking shorter strokes, and tried to maintain control over her rampaging libido. It was difficult with the clit massager buzzing enthusiastically and her sucking cock. She had always found fellatio enthralling, a profound manner in which to serve.

The vibrator quieted. Lillian clawed for control over herself and swallowed Alek again. She peeked up at him with the expectation he'd be watching her with his typical in-control domineering expression.

He looked at her, all right, but his countenance was different. He still appeared strong, unflappable, but there was…warmth? Something in his gaze she hadn't seen before. A sort of softness. Whatever it was, it made her stomach flutter. A surge of gratitude to be kneeling before him, permitted to suck his cock, swept over Lillian. As if being his wasn't merely a scene to be played for her sexual satisfaction, but real.

It was the advanced program. It had brought in the interactive nuances. *Damn, we did an amazing job on that.*

Before she could think about it further, the vibrator switched on again. With a moan, she allowed most of his shaft to slip out.

Alek wrapped his hands around her head, holding her immobile. He fucked her mouth. He forced her to take him deep with every thrust. The clit massager felt as if it wouldn't ever stop, and Lillian's attention focused on keeping climax at bay, on swallowing and holding her breath, on being Alek's good, obedient slave.

Her trembling became quaking as orgasm threatened. Just as Lillian felt she couldn't hold off any longer, the vibrator fell quiet.

Alek chose that moment to withdraw. Without a word, he stooped and put his shoulder against her middle. He stood, lifting her so she draped, her face against his back.

He smacked her rear as he bore her toward the fuck chair. She yelped at the stinging pain, then groaned as the massager switched on again. Jupiter's storm, she was dying to come.

Alek settled her on the fuck chair, as she'd suspected he would. The black leather chair, with its multitudes of straps and restraints, had been a design project between the two of them, built to their specifications. The seat was firm with no give, and Lillian squirmed as her weight settled on her poor, sensitive ass.

Alek pinched her nipple in punishment. "Problem, slave?"

"No sir," she moaned as sharp agony lanced from her tit. "I'm sorry."

"Behave or you'll go in the cage for the rest of the night."

Lillian glanced at the wire enclosure he referred to. That particular contraption had been one of her worst ideas, especially when she was desperately aroused, as she was at that moment. In the cage, manacled to its crossbars, Alek would torment her with fucking, vibrators, anything that he felt would punish her...and deny her orgasm no matter how much she begged.

She whimpered another apology.

He stripped her of the clit massager. With her already well bound, Alek only needed to strap her legs in position: black restraints that circled her legs above her knees and secured them to the top of the chair. Her hips were tilted forward, her knees bent to her ears, her legs spread to afford access to her pussy and ass...to anything it suited him to take. He tilted the chair back forty-five degrees, and raised it to his crotch level.

Alek looked her over. She semi-reclined, her arms tied so her breasts were lifted, thrusting upward. Legs wide and bent, displaying her wantonly. His gaze held weight, especially as the seconds ticked by and he didn't move.

Alek, in sexual master mode, had an evaluating stare that held no emotion. Lillian was used to that; she rather enjoyed it, actually. It allowed her to dive deeper into the fantasy she was his to do with as he chose.

He didn't look any different from their earlier trysts. On the surface, he was the same old Master Alek who put her through her paces in so many delightful, dirty ways. Yet she sensed a greater attention than usual…more of an assessment. As if her appearance deserved greater contemplation than in the past.

He murmured under his breath, a hint of syllables that she caught only the barest trace of. Had he muttered beautiful?

Alek shook his head and stepped forward. His cock, incredibly warm, pressed against her wet cunt. Lillian exhaled and forced herself to relax. Experience told her what was coming.

He took her in a single thrust. Her pussy clenched at the incredible incursion and exalted in the mingled pain and bliss of the abrupt invasion. For a moment, Lillian feared she would come despite his demand she hold off. Her sex seized on his, only an instant, a mere fraction of a movement from explosion.

Alek paused, his groin tight to hers. He stared hard at her. Daring her to disobey. She groaned a wordless plea, whether for the mercy of climax or his understanding, she wasn't sure.

The near-climax hesitated, then retreated. Not far; she remained in danger of losing control. She shuddered under the dual threats of rampant arousal and her master's displeasure.

As she relaxed, Alek's unsparing stare eased. His features softened for only a second, gone so quickly, she realized she must have imagined it. His vise pinch to her nipples punished her for her momentary lack of control, and she wailed an apology.

He fucked her. His body slapped against hers with the forceful, determined thrusts she relished. He rutted hard enough to make her grunt with each shove deep within. He gripped her breasts as he did so, squeezing the flesh so it leaked between his fingers.

"Beg for it," he snarled.

"Fuck me, Master, fuck your slave, fuck this slave's pussy, please, fuck me hard." She didn't have to pretend she meant it.

"Keep going."

"Fuck me until I can't walk, fill me with all your hot cum, I only exist to serve you, please, Master, please!" She writhed beneath him as much as her bonds granted. Her voice rose louder as he plunged and plunged and plunged between her legs.

"Do you wish to come for me, slave?"

"Yes, Master! For you!"

"For no one else? Only me?" His gaze grew more intense.

"Only you, always you, please, Master!" Climax threatened again. It nipped at her and tried to force itself on her.

"Then do so." To add emphasis to his long-awaited permission, he pinched her clit.

Delicious, hurtful bliss barreled through her, lighting fireworks. Lillian screamed with the force of ecstasy as it exploded and tore her inside out.

A telltale pulse added to her rapture. Alek grunted. His demanding expression melted into a sudden slackening of his features. He'd released the fake semen stored in his sack and filled her with warmth. He overflowed her cunt with a generous release, at least half of what his balls contained.

His obvious pleasure added to Lillian's. Not for the first time was she grateful the cyborgs' manufacturers had given them the ability to appreciate physical sensation.

She was still spasming with the last surges of passion when Alek pulled out, both his cock and the plug in her ass.

She floated until she received a demanding shove against her back hole again.

Her master was far from done with her. He bored into her and forced her to yield to his demand. Her ass had been stretched by the generous girth of the plug, but Alek was far bigger. An ache announced itself as he insisted she submit. The air filled with her female cries and his animal grunts.

He patted her pussy as he delved deep. It wasn't a harsh slap, but it wasn't gentle either. Most of the contact landed on her swollen, sensitive clit. Lillian shouted as hurt and passion combined into a single eager drive, and she climaxed again.

Her world tossed and turned as Alek drove into her with insistence. He continued the firm taps to her rioting clit. Explosive orgasm shredded her and renewed its strength when Alek's cock jerked again and emptied into her ass. Lillian rode the maelstrom until its final sweet ebb.

When she sighed and blinked herself free of the post-coital high, she discovered Alek watched her. A slight smile warmed his handsome face. "I haven't heard you yell that loud in a while. Shall we call the shibari program a success?"

She grinned. "Sure, but a lot of that had more to do with the knot tyer than the knots themselves. You were amazing, Alek. You get better all the time."

"I'm glad you enjoyed it. Do you want water or untying first?"

"Water. And some pain meds. I'm going to be a wreck when the endorphin high fades."

"You got it." He started to leave to fetch what she needed, then hesitated. Alek looked her over again, then kissed each of her nipples wetly.

"Don't get me started again," Lillian pleaded as excitement zinged from his touch to her pussy. "I can't handle anymore tonight."

He chuckled and bestowed an identical kiss to her clit before heading to the kitchen for water. "I'll take that as a compliment."

* * * *

Lillian let Alek pilot the shuttle to work the next morning. She was still recovering from the intense sex of the night before…along with a pronounced lack of sleep. As much as he'd exhausted her, her brain had refused to shut off for more than an hour or two of slumber. She'd wakened to think and fret no less than half a dozen times.

For some reason, the combination of telling Alek about her failed romances, his listening with seeming understanding and sympathy, then the mind-blowing sex that had felt more intense than usual…it messed with her that morning. She wasn't sure why, but she felt as if a seismic change had happened between them.

The possibility bothered her. The idea they'd edged close on an emotional level, entirely feasible now with Alek's enhanced interpersonal program, had her eager to put distance between them. It didn't matter that the feelings she worried most about hadn't been the those she found threatening.

Certainly, there was no love between her and Alek. No actual closeness. Affection? Sure, of the friendly, year-long acquaintance type. A comfortableness since Alek was a known quantity. And of course, lust. He knew everything about her when it came to what got her off, and he performed without error.

Why was she feeling so crazy? So…vulnerable?

It made no sense, particularly since he'd done nothing to break the silence of their morning commute. He wasn't even looking at her. He was Alek-As-Usual, navigating the routes along the interior of ring-shaped Alpha Station's collection of units, performing his assigned duty of piloting. Nothing more.

Of course he's acting normal. Nothing's changed. Stop being weird.

Easier thought than done.

She kept herself from sighing with relief as they flew into CyberServe's vast portion of Alpha Space Station and landed in its docking bay. At work, there'd be no cause to worry Alek would behave in any way but his usual professional self as her assistant.

Except he was also her bodyguard. He insisted she remain on the shuttle while he had a look around the bay. In the mood she was in, Lillian was less than happy to be ordered around by her company's cyborg. She had to remind herself he was behaving as he should after an assassination attempt against her. She needed to pull her shit together.

"Seems clear," he reported through the open hatch. "You can come out now."

Biting off an inappropriate retort, Lillian exited the shuttle and followed him into CyberServe.

After they entered her office, Alek sat at his desk and began his day, as if it were any other. The police had gathered whatever evidence they'd found, and maintenance had cleaned the room. There was no sign of the horrific events from the morning before.

Lillian ordered coffee. She confirmed her most pressing tasks and upcoming appointments with Alek. Made the calls she needed to. She settled as life took up its usual rhythms. *Nothing to see here, folks.*

If Alek seemed a little quieter than usual, she chalked it up to playing catchup. Appointments of the day before had to be rescheduled, missed work hurriedly accomplished, and present assignments attacked. Lillian wondered if he appreciated the extra effort that absorbed their attention and sped the hours past. She certainly did.

She went out to lunch with him hovering close to keep her safe. Their conversation was no different from any other day. They focused on that afternoon's showroom meeting with a celebrity who was interested in buying a cyborg assistant.

"A pool boy and man about the house." She smirked as she dug into her salad.

"Usually code for a sex toy cyborg." Alek chuckled as he looked around the quiet restaurant.

His expression of humor halted her fork's progress halfway to her mouth. Lillian shook off the surprise. He had the full advanced interaction program. It was natural he would laugh. The situation warranted it.

"After over a dozen well-publicized relationships and breakups, half of which resulted in tell-all interviews from her exes, can you blame Lady Leona?" Lillian could sympathize. Hell yes, sell that woman a cyborg who'd keep its mouth shut. Let her have her fun without worrying about tabloids.

They returned to the office as soon as she finished eating. The instant she brought her computer online, a message popped up.

Your days are numbered, cyborg slut.

Chapter Six

"Um, Alek? I have a love note here."

He hurried over and scowled at the words floating on the monitor. "Gunnar Jax. Or someone from the Freedom League."

"Wouldn't they have had to come in here and access my computer in person to leave a note on it?"

"Not necessarily, though I'll check the security feeds. It could be Cruz got hold of your access codes and passed them on to his co-conspirators before he tried to kill you." He tapped the inter-company communicator.

"Michaels here."

"This is Alek, assistant to Mr. Kwolek. Security Chief, I need you to run a scan on electronic relays. See if a piggyback signal diverter is present on any of them. Probably homemade." As he spoke, Alek returned to his own computer and typed busily.

"Commencing scan. Is there a problem, Alek?"

"A nasty message has been left on the president's main screen. I'm contacting law enforcement and checking my personal security monitors for possible egress into Mr. Kwolek's office. There seems to have been none. I'm assuming the message was sent from a remote location."

"You were right. My scans show a device on the relay nearest to the president's office. It looks pretty crude. I'm sending a detail to retrieve it for law enforcement."

"Excellent job, Mr. Michaels. When the officers arrive, show them to the president's office."

Lillian grimaced at Alek as he clicked the connection off. "How likely are we to find proof it's the Freedom League?"

"Not much."

She sighed. "I'll have to postpone this afternoon's meeting with Ursa Leona. I hope we don't lose this sale."

As it turned out, Ursa Leona was running late herself. The opera star had been held up at her lawyer's office to "settle a matter of great importance." Lillian hoped it had to do with a show contract instead of having to fend off another scandalous tell-all. Lady Leona had been through another public breakup the month before.

The diva arrived minutes after Officers Kahn and Stillman left with the remote transmitter they'd agreed had probably been installed by Cruz. There'd been little else police could do about the threat beyond adding it to the case.

Lillian set aside the latest harassment and hurried to the showroom to greet Lady Ursa Leona with Alek on her heels.

"A most appreciated welcome. This was exactly what I needed," their hoped-for client greeted them in the small lounge outside the showroom. The black-haired soprano raised her half-full champagne flute to them.

"Welcome to CyberServe, Lady Leona. We're honored you're considering one of our life assistants."

"Is this one of your exquisite cyborgs? He's handsome fellow." Ursa raked Alek with her gaze.

"My assistant, Alek. He's indeed a wonderful representative of the PSM line of cyborgs."

He bowed from the waist rather than his head, an old-fashioned greeting Ursa appeared to appreciate. "Is there anything I can fetch you besides the champagne, Lady Leona? We have a number of hors d'ouevres, from sweet to savory."

"Thank you, Alek, but no. I'm somewhat unsettled. Meetings with lawyers have that effect." She unfolded herself from the chair. Rings glittered from every finger when she waved her flute. "I don't suppose I could beg a top-off?"

"You beg for nothing." He smiled.

Lillian eyed him with amusement as he waved to the steward they called in for such occasions. He'd never been so suave. The interactive program upgrade had unleashed a new salesman in Alek. He had Ursa fawning over him, when she was usually the person others fawned over.

After re-filling her flute, they moved on to the showroom. The display area was bright and shiny, a twinkling masterpiece. Gleaming white walls, floor, and ceiling. Glittering computer banks, where techs stood at various stations, dressed in white suits and white lab coats. And all around, waiting for inspection, the dressed-to-impress cyborgs stood on separate round pedestals.

Ursa breathed in, at last distracted from Alek to take in his fellows. "Oh my. What a spectacular selection."

"These are merely samples. Some alterations can be applied to the facial structure. Hair and eye color can also be tailored to your preferences."

"Yes, of course. I've seen your promotions. It's just in person...they take the breath away, don't they?"

Lillian did her best not to swell with pride. "Indeed, they do. Would you like an escort, or do you prefer to browse on your own?"

"Let me wander and absorb them."

"Gladly. If you have any questions, my techs and I stand ready to assist you. If you wish to speak with a cyborg, they'll be powered up to do so."

"These already have programs installed?"

"Low-level advanced personal interaction software. They won't be quite as personable as Alek, but you'll get a hint of temperament and character. With your own, you'll be able to download as high a level as suits you."

Ursa began her tour. She paused before each cyborg, whether male or female. She was fascinated, which Lillian judged a good sign for a quick sale.

"Bets?" she whispered to Alek as soon as the opera diva was out of earshot.

"Hmm. Judging by her past lovers and husbands, I'll wager on the SIM. She appreciates the suave, elegant, debonair type."

"A former infiltrator and spy unit, huh?"

"What do you think?"

"I'd agree, but I'm certain you impressed her. I'm betting on the PSM model."

An hour later, after touring the room twice and speaking to half a dozen cyborgs, Ursa returned to Lillian. "I've chosen."

"Wonderful!" Lillian had begun to think the singer wasn't ready to buy after all. "Who's the lucky cyborg going home with you?"

"The SIM. He's so classy."

Alek winked at Lillian over Ursa's shoulder and grinned ear to ear. Smug bastard.

Their earlier guess the client was planning on more than pool boy duties for her purchase was confirmed as the opera star chose significant alterations to the cyborg's appearance and paid a chunk of money for the all-inclusive software package. Mechasexual romance was in the air. Such clients almost never bought the individual sex programs. They preferred to hide their intentions by plunking down the big bucks for access to everything.

"That'll be the cleanest damn swimming pool on Alpha Station," Alek snickered after Ursa left with her new cyborg an hour later.

MINE TO KEEP

Lillian laughed so hard, she nearly fell on her ass. The showroom techs, filing out now that the performance was over, glanced at her.

"Ah, people are wonderful. Cyborgs doubly so," she sighed.

"Appreciation is a wonderful thing," Alek grinned. His hand brushed hers. "Tell me more about how wonderful I am."

She swallowed. Something in his gaze reminded her of the night before, just as she had put it behind her.

She was reluctant to quit the showroom for some reason. She wandered the aisles between the silent, unpowered demo models and considered. She stopped in front of a SIM model, similar to that which had won Ursa's affections.

The Infiltrator was indeed an elegant stunner. Nowhere as muscled as Lillian preferred, but shaped perfectly for the tuxedo he wore. Trim. Graceful. His facial structure and smart hairstyle screamed sophistication.

"You know, I've never tried out one of these. They're, what, the third-best seller among the male models?"

"The female versions of the Infiltrator are the most popular of that gender." The laughter had left Alek's voice.

"The female models are a teenage boy's wet dream. As well as a middle-aged man who feels his youth slipping away." She glanced at the nearest showroom SIF and felt a twinge of jealousy. Most female clients did. Wasp-thin waist, boobs as big as Lillian's, and a truckload of ass. The male customers, attended by a salesman rather than Lillian, made no bones about cherry-picking the sex program when they purchased a SIF. They were built for lustful fantasies, which had aided the model's original spy programming.

Lillian returned her attention to the SIF's male counterpart. He put her in mind of the classic movie gentleman spy at the card table. He looked like the kind of secret agent who beguiled the female enemy to join him in his bed before they commenced trying to kill each other.

"Yeah. I'm overdue to give this guy a whirl." She went to the computer station to power him up.

"I'll be going home with you too." Alek stayed where he was, though his gaze followed her. "To keep an eye on security."

Lillian kept her eyes on the computer before her. She reached for the power button that would activate the SIM. "I guess you'll appreciate me not bothering you with my demands as I did last night then." It would also put her back on familiar footing with Alek.

"I was perfectly fine with your demands." His mutter was just loud enough to hear.

Chapter Seven

Alek listened to the sounds coming from the playroom as he paced the condo. He pretended to patrol. He pretended he wasn't pacing to shed the churning feeling in his gut.

Flesh slapped flesh, followed by agonized cries. He did his best to avoid guessing if Lillian was draped over the bench, bound to the x-cross, or over the Infiltrator's lap as the other cyborg spanked her. He tried to avoid thoughts about any of it.

She'd enjoyed the night before. It had been their best playtime yet. He was certain of it. Nonetheless, she'd brought that stupid little fop of a SIM home to give her the painful exhilaration she couldn't get enough of. That overdressed, skinny cyborg—

"Bet his cock's as thin as the rest of him," Alek muttered to himself. "Bet she won't even feel it when he sticks it in her tight little ass."

That brought a vision of the Infiltrator performing the act, and he ground his teeth together.

The matrix has identified extreme input in the circuits. An analysis suggests strong emotion. Would the unit describe the feeling for analysis?

"No. Be quiet until I ask for an opinion."

He was well aware of what the terrible sensation was. He'd seen it and heard about it from many sources during the year since he'd been activated.

He was jealous. Which suggested his enhanced programming had altered from seeing Lillian as a supervisor and subject to be protected. He'd begun to regard her as more. It was exactly what he'd hoped to avoid when she'd upgraded his interactive program.

He disliked it. It was as ugly as the fear he'd learned when he'd downloaded the security program.

Interspersed with obsessing with the unwanted feelings was the experience itself. Why would she choose the Infiltrator over him? Was it because she hated involvement with anyone after the poor relationships she'd attempted before? Was it fear Alek would hurt her as the other men had?

He wasn't attracted to other women though. He couldn't even imagine it. Ursa had flirted with him, and he hadn't felt a thing beyond a slight sense of amusement and flattery. Only Lillian's regard interested him.

Maybe he'd behaved too charmingly. He'd researched Ursa Leona when she'd contacted CyberServe for an appointment to review cyborgs for a possible purchase. What he'd learned about the potentially lucrative client for CyberServe had revealed she'd respond best to courtly behavior. His actions toward the famous soprano had been all about the sale. Had Lillian taken it the wrong way? Had she suspected he'd been attracted to another female?

Alek decided the answer was no after careful contemplation. Nothing in her manner had suggested anything but humor at his actions. In fact, it had been the only instance that day when she hadn't displayed any sort of tension.

Her reaction had to be from concern he'd turn his new emotions into more than she wished. If she found out he was jealous, it would confirm her fears.

He passed the closed door to the playroom and bared his teeth when he heard a sly chuckle and a feminine murmur.

Jealousy. That was what he felt, and he wanted it to go away.

His matrix must have regarded the thought as a request for response. *You might find a hobby to distract yourself. A new person to focus your attention on. In the case of extreme jealousy, surrender yourself to a programmer for a memory wipe and reboot.*

He snorted. He was gaining emotions, and the matrix was ill-prepared to help him cope. Still, he was curious about its advisory.

What constitutes extreme jealousy?

A wish to harm others, whether it's the unit's focus object of affection or the threat to the unit's focus object of affection. If this unit wishes to injure or kill anyone or to destroy property as a consequence of jealousy, the unit must surrender for memory wipe and reboot.

He mused over the information. He had no wish to wound anyone or anything, even the stupid Infiltrator fucking Lillian. After all, the Infiltrator was merely a sex tool at the moment. Programmed at the most basic level, it was no more than a walking, talking, rutting vibrator. As for Lillian…well, the idea of hurting her made his circuits whine as much as the jealousy did.

A sense of heaviness joined the electric sizzle of jealousy and anger. He felt weighted as he performed another circuit of the condo, and asked the matrix about it.

Analysis: depression. Sadness. Unhappiness. Would the unit like a list of possible remedies for this state?

"I'd like to have never been re-activated."

* * * *

Lillian followed Alek through the halls of CyberServe the next morning. The smile she wore to greet her employees was tight and unnatural as she responded to their acknowledgments.

Her mood was shitty. Not bad, not grumpy, not sullen. Shitty.

The Infiltrator, which she'd sent to the showroom with instructions to resume its post on its dais and shut itself down, had been a major disappointment. Sure, he'd done everything by the book...by the program. Yes, she'd gotten off multiple times. She was one of those rare, lucky women who could climax simply due to her vivid imagination. She believed she'd have to be on her deathbed before her lively libido failed her. But sex with the SIM had been a letdown.

Hell, it had been as shitty as her mood. The Infiltrator's low-level basic interpersonal setting had been devoid of feeling compared to Alek. His expressions, whether demanding or approving, had possessed an odd, plastic quality. His tone rarely varied, which had rendered "Behave or I'll punish you" no more compelling than "I'd better order some milk from the store." He'd stopped often to ask if he was punishing her at an adequate level.

Lillian regarded Alek from behind. For all her worries about emotional complications with him, she had to admit his upgrades and history with her rendered a major difference. Sex play with him was more intense. More real.

I don't want real. Real means trouble. Real means hurt and betrayal.

She liked Alek, far more than was safe. She was willing to admit that, at least to herself. But no man...no cyborg, for that matter...would ever break her heart again.

* * * *

Lillian had managed to get through half the morning, mostly in silence shared by Alek, when the cyborg got up from his desk and came over to stand in front of hers. "President Kwolek, if I may have a word?"

Startled by the formality, she gaped at him. "Of course, Alek.

"I request permission to uninstall the interpersonal program."

"But the feedback issue…isn't that still a concern?"

His lips thinned. "I'm willing to risk it."

"I'm not." She scowled, hiding her sinking heart with anger. "You're too important to the company to endanger yourself."

"Lillian—"

"I can grab another cyborg to assume security duties. Removing the bodyguard program might help whatever concerns you're having."

"I wish to return to how I was before. The lesser degree of interpersonal programming. The…the lack of emotions." Alek's fists clenched. His jaw tightened.

"Are you angry with me?" she asked. Disbelief warred with what she saw before her.

His tension eased and made way for pleading. "Of course not. But surely you can see I don't function correctly since the upgrade."

"I thought you were doing fine."

"I was jealous last night. I intensely disliked that you had sex with the Infiltrator."

She stared at him. He'd been jealous she'd played with the SIM? Alek? *But I didn't even enjoy it*. On the heels of that, chagrin washed over her. She'd probably hurt his feelings to boot. He'd been walloped by emotions while she'd been going out of her way to protect hers.

"I'm sorry," she said softly. "It wasn't my intention to upset you. I was…I wanted to…"

"You needed space. Or to let me know I shouldn't get attached." He shrugged. "I would have been pleased if it had succeeded."

Why was she overwhelmed with guilt? It wasn't her fault his damned program had gone overboard and set off an emotional connection. She'd been as reluctant as he to install the upgrade in the first place.

It made sense to give him what he asked for, to disable the interpersonal program. She should do so and have a new bodyguard occupy his place. There was no reason why she shouldn't. Lillian and Alek could return to how they'd been before the Freedom League had begun to harass her.

All it would require was an order. *Revert to previous programming.*

There was a curious blockage in her throat. Solid resistance to speaking the command. She struggled against it, but it refused to budge.

"I...I'm...are you sure, Alek? I mean, there's no one I trust as much as I trust you."

"I'm not meant for these moods," he groaned. "I don't understand how you humans can stand it. There's no good to be had from them."

Just let the poor guy go back to who he was. But the words wouldn't come.

"I understand what you're saying. I really do. But I have these meetings today, and you have to be there. It would take time to get another cyborg up to speed where security is concerned. Time we don't have right now."

He grimaced. "That's true. I'll consult the schedule, check on when I can clear a few hours to take care of it. Tomorrow's the weekend. Hopefully, sometime next week—" He broke off and went to his desk.

Yes. Next week. That gave her a few nights to sleep on it, to figure out why doing what she should was so damned difficult.

Analyze the ongoing feedback loop issue. Is it confirmed there's nothing cataclysmically wrong with this unit?
Analysis: there is no current feedback loop issue.
The moods are too strong. They're increasing.
The unit is coping within normal parameters. Factors increasing emotional awakening are familiarity with Lillian Kwolek after a year of intense interaction, coupled with enhanced interactive programming. The unit's concern is invalid.

Alek kept himself from swearing as he juggled the day's tasks. He focused on his work, aware of Lillian's gaze on him.

As he'd requested the programming downgrade and faced the fact she would have to use a different cyborg as a bodyguard, the awful emotions had surged.

Another cyborg in her home. Another cyborg watching over her, one that didn't know her as well as he did. Couldn't know her, even with his help.

Another cyborg. Not him.

He'd lose the attentive feelings for her that were waking. That was exactly what he'd thought he wanted. But all at once, the notion made him feel worse. Too not experience anything when he gazed at her…?

Like most of the emotions that rampaged through him, the warmth when he looked at Lillian was disconcerting. It was unnerving, but pleasant. Enthralling, even.

I care. She means something to me.
Analysis: affection. Fondness. Devo—
Shut up. On the heels of that, he asked the matrix, *do other awakened cyborgs struggle with this?*
Define 'struggle.'
Do they hate their emotions? Do they want them to stop?

Central Processing and Records indicates five purchased cyborgs have returned for memory erasures, citing an inability to properly manage emotions.

Five out of how many purchased assistants?

Twelve hundred fifty-seven.

Five out of...that's all? So emotional confusion is rare. Yet you say I'm coping within parameters.

Twelve hundred fifty-seven is the total number of cyborgs sold to this date. The number of cyborgs that have self-actualized is unknown, due to a lack of consistent reporting from owners. With that information unavailable, it must be assumed the majority consider their emotions uncomfortable but manage them successfully.

Alek frowned. Why wasn't CyberServe keeping records of the number of fully realized cyborgs? He didn't dare ask Lillian about it with the air so full of tension.

Why didn't the five cyborgs have the interactive programs downgraded? Or removed?

Three of the five did. Emotional realization was unaffected.

Alek stilled. *Downgrading the interactive program failed to halt their ability to react with sentiment?*

Affirmative. Only wiping the units' memories and starting from a blank slate cured the passions they were unable to cope with.

Was that what Alek would have to do to fix the mess he was in? Delete everything he'd learned in the past year? Destroy who he'd become to find peace?

It would mean erasing Lillian from his circuits. Making it as if he'd never known her.

Lillian stared at her monitor, blind to the cost analyses floating before her eyes.

You hurt Alek.

He was supposed to be just a bodyguard. Just an assistant. Just an occasional fuck.

He's discovered feelings for you.

She couldn't allow it. If he could care about her, if he could suffer jealousy over her, he could find someone else to direct those emotions toward. He could hurt her.

The way you hurt him last night.

She hadn't meant to. She hadn't known, damn it.

You took that pathetic Infiltrator home to put distance between yourself and Alek.

Why? If she'd had no idea that he was developing the emotions he was, why had she done it?

You know why.

Impossible.

She had to figure out the situation. She had the weekend coming up with Alek, because she needed him to keep her safe from Gunnar Jax and his lunatics. A whole weekend. With Alek. Who'd just asked her to uninstall programming so he could go back to being an unfeeling cyborg. A mere tool. Which was what he was. Right?

The mocking voice in her head laughed. *How long have you been lying to yourself about how you regard him?*

She saw him as a cyborg. Nothing more.

Why did you name him, then? Why did you personalize an object? A machine? A 'mere tool,' as you put it?

* * * *

Lillian had no idea if she was relieved to head home that evening or if she dreaded it. Alek was morose, barely speaking to her. Which should have been a relief. She had no idea what to say to him.

It was stacking up to be a long weekend.

Last-minute issues with an atmosphere-control failure in cyborg storage had kept them busy up to quitting time. Lillian and Alek had scrambled to find a new system for the huge space. Replacing the skin of tens of thousands of cyborgs would have cost CyberServe an enormous amount of time and money. And clients. Fortunately, the maintenance crew had vacuum-sealed the chamber quickly, keeping damage from occurring until the arrival of the company Lillian had hired to spend the weekend repairing or replacing the warehouse's atmospheric system. Even a full replacement added to emergency and overtime fees would cost less than growing collagen sheets to cover all those cyborg metal chassis.

At least dealing with the abrupt death of the atmosphere controls had distracted her from the coming days she'd have to spend with Alek. Alek, who wanted to erase his awakening attachment to her. Alek, whom she was now following to the shuttle bay.

They didn't speak. She was afraid to glance at him, afraid she'd see another flash of anger. Or dread. Or hurt over what she'd done the night before.

He walked faster than her, putting distance between them. She let him.

The hall was empty. Quiet reigned on the executive floor for the most part, compared to the usual noise of employees bustling about during the height of the day. She heard a few distant voices, but most had headed out early, ready for a couple days away from the office.

She was startled when the blue-carpeted floor under her shining oxfords thrummed. Then it trembled. It shook. It quaked as rumbling thunder exploded through the air. Through her confusion, she saw Alek stagger forward a few steps, his arms pinwheeling as he fought to catch his balance.

The corridor was rising, leaving the walls behind. No, that wasn't right. The walls were falling, crumbling around her. A great chunk smashed to the floor between her and Alek, and dust hid him from her sight. She shouted and staggered along the bucking ground, fighting to get past the debris, to make sure he hadn't been hit.

The floor beneath her heaved, throwing her forward with violence, as if she'd been shot from a cannon. She landed hard, and pieces of the ceiling rained down on her. She cried out as pain walloped her.

There was a second of silence. Everything stopped moving, and she stared upward at the torn ceiling overhead. A metal conduit, round and serpentine, snaked overhead. She lay stunned, listening as noise began again, the rumble of large objects sliding, the tumble of smaller objects rolling across uneven surfaces. And screams.

She was moving. So was everything else around her, all the fragments of walls and ceiling. Tugged by an irresistible force that pulled her down the corridor. She slid with the rest of the rubble across the floor, heading down the hall in a bizarre imitation of riding a playground slide, except she was horizontal. She shouldn't be sliding. Why was she sliding?

It came to her in a rush. There'd been a hull fracture. Sudden decompression. She was being sucked to wherever the hole was.

Sucked into space.

Chapter Eight

"Lillian!"

An arm waved from a doorway. Alek hung on to its frame as she slid past, his features hectic with determination. He lunged for her and missed. He swung out farther, hanging onto the doorframe by his fingertips. He managed to grab her wrist and halted her unintended exit. Despite the determined pull that stretched her, straining her from the arm he gripped, she went no further.

He hauled her to the office door of a junior executive. He expended little effort to do so. As a cyborg, metal under the skin, his strength overwhelmed the vacuum. He pulled her into himself and protected her from flying debris. Alek clasped her to his chest and flung them both into the dimly lit office. He triggered the door shut.

She gasped, too shocked to speak. Too shocked to keep him from holding her upright, stunned at the sudden silence after the tumult of objects being dragged out to space. She was still trying to gather her scattered thoughts when Alek cursed and cupped her chin. He held her so he could look into her face.

"Are you all right? No, you're not. Let me see." He shoved aside her jacket, yanked the knot of her tie loose, and popped several buttons ripping her shirt off to inspect her bleeding shoulder. "This isn't too bad. Let me look at the rest of you."

He carried her to the desk and sat her on its surface. She thought dimly she should protest his stripping her to the waist to search for injuries, but she wasn't sure why. Then he pulled her pants down. He found a few more cuts on her legs.

"Nothing life threatening. I'll check for a first aid kit and clean you up." He hurried to the attached lavatory, leaving her shivering, naked but for her trousers bunched around her shoes.

Some sense reasserted itself. "Alek? What happened? Was it a hull breach?"

"Seems so." He returned with a wet cloth and the first aid kit.

"We need to call for help. What if—will we have enough oxygen?"

"I don't need it." He nodded to the emergency oxygen tanks and masks behind its glass case in the wall. Every office had two, and many more were located at regular intervals along the halls, as mandated by the ITCS. "You're set if levels drop inside this room, but closing the door should have sealed the air in. Hear the air exchangers?" He nodded at the vent in the ceiling.

Lillian knew all that. She realized she was panicking in the wake of what had happened. She forced herself to breathe normally. She was safe. Help would come soon, because sudden decompression would send alerts to emergency personnel. Better yet, she had Alek.

"The power's still on." The lights, set on dim due to the office's occupant leaving for the day, worked fine. The whisper of the air exchanger was constant. "Did it feel like an explosion to you?"

"Felt and sounded like it." He bandaged her shoulder, the worst of her injuries, and gazed into her eyes. "You're okay?"

"I'm fine. Sorry I got a little rattled there." She scowled at herself.

He choked a laugh. "Even presidents of major corporations are allowed to go into shock when their surroundings fall apart and they're nearly dragged into space."

"Alek, there were others on this floor. I heard them screaming."

His expression turned grim. "I heard them too. Let me see if I can raise anyone in Security to check. I have to let them know where we are so we can be rescued."

A minute later, as Alek worked on the cuts on Lillian's legs, Michaels spoke to them over the in-house system. "The explosion came from the executive shuttle bay, there on your level. That's where the worst destruction is, with the levels below and above sustaining damage too, though they didn't suffer a breach. It's just the two of you?"

"Yes, but we know there were others still working on this level. We have no idea if they reached safety." Lillian winced as Alek applied antiseptic to her shin, but her tone remained level. He grimaced an apology.

"Rescue crews are less than a minute from arrival. I've informed them where you're sheltering, so they should get to you pretty quick. Meanwhile, I'm reviewing video footage to see if we can locate other survivors."

"Due to the problems we've had lately, this needs to be treated as potential terrorism. Despite the extra safeguards put in place for the shuttle bay, my first thought is someone snuck a bomb in." The notion churned her stomach, but Lillian wouldn't hide behind wishful thinking.

"It could have been flown in on an employee's vessel. I went over the executive staff's history and found nothing suspect, but…well, it's no use guessing. I'll do what it takes to assist law enforcement find out if we have another saboteur. A rescue shuttle is hailing me. Hang in there; help is coming. Michaels out."

Alek finished bandaging and managed a weak smile. "Glue, twine, and duct tape. You're put together again."

"Jupiter's storm, Alek. If it weren't for you—"

Lillian slung her arms around his neck and yanked him close. She buried her face against his shoulder and was comforted when he embraced her tightly. Whether either of them wanted to care for the other or not, she was glad at that moment that they did.

* * * *

"Definitely an explosive. Definitely near, perhaps aboard, a particular shuttle parked in the executive bay," Kahn said two hours later. She leaned back in her chair. "Maybe in it. Maybe attached to it. The owner might have been unaware it was there."

"Either way, it flew through the security field without tripping the alarm," Stillman added from his desk, a few feet away. "Someone knew what they were doing."

"Our investigation will determine exactly what happened. Meanwhile, we're having a team search your condo building to make sure nothing else blows up in your vicinity."

"Thanks." Lillian sipped stale, lukewarm coffee in the pair's office for something to do. She put the cup on Kahn's desk and braced herself for the answer to the question she hated to ask. "Any idea how many of my employees were…were dragged out?"

Kahn sighed. "Five confirmed dead on the premises. Nine more were picked up on the monitors going through the hole in the hull. Sweepers have picked up four of those so far. Seven are missing, but there was nearly a minute where the bay cameras were knocked out of commission by the blast before they resumed transmission. The missing may have been the first to go."

Lillian covered her face and moaned. The news hit her in the gut with the force of a physical blow. "Nearly two dozen?" Two dozen dead. On her watch.

"Out of nearly three hundred who work on that level alone? It could have been much worse."

"Tell that to their families."

Alek gripped Lillian's shoulder. "It's bad, there's no getting past it. But at least it happened just before the weekend, when so many sneak off a few minutes early. Otherwise, the numbers would have been catastrophic."

She drew a shuddering breath and came out from behind her hands. "I guess we have to take the good news where we can get it."

It sure as hell didn't feel like good news.

Alek grasped her statement, held it close to his chaotic feelings. The good news, at least for him, was worth celebrating.

He'd watched Lillian being dragged off, toward likely death. He'd almost missed catching her as the vacuum had pulled her away. The fact he could have been destroyed too, though he might have survived being flung into space…it would have depended on how violently…paled next to the certainty she wouldn't have.

As they rose to go home, his arm curled around her. Protectively, yes, keeping her safe was uppermost in his mind, but also because he required the contact. He could see her, smell her perfume, hear her speak her thanks and farewells to Kahn and Stillman, but he needed to feel her too.

I almost lost her.

He couldn't wrap his mind around that. It wasn't possible he could exist in a galaxy absent Lillian Kwolek.

Analysis of this inclination.

State inclination.
Existence isn't worthwhile without Lillian Kwolek.
Analysis: Strong attachment. The unit shows signs of falling in love.
Exactly the emotion he'd most feared.

* * * *

Lillian's shuttle had been damaged during the blast and after it had been tossed violently into space, according to the debris sweeper company which had picked it up and towed it to a salvage yard. She accepted a ride home for herself and Alek from a patrol officer. Her condo sector had been investigated for explosives by the police and given the all clear, fortunately. She wanted nothing but to shut herself in her home and hide from the hostile universe.

Once she stepped through the condo's door, she wandered from room to room. Her surroundings made no impression on her. Away from the distraction of Kahn's and Stillman's questions and reports, the latest attack replayed itself in her head over and over.

CyberServe shaking. Debris falling. An irresistible forcing dragging her down the hall. The final screams of the lost. Alek reaching for her, his eyes wide with terror, his lips forming her name.

"Easy. Lillian, sit down. You're in shock." His muscled arm surrounded her shoulders, and he wiped dry the tears she hadn't realized she'd been crying.

"I'm fine. I'm fine." She pushed against his chest and resisted the urge to crumble into his embrace.

She wouldn't let herself rely on him. She could get along okay without him. She'd done so for years, never dependent on others. She was strong. Self-sufficient.

But those screams. Alek's terrified stare that announced her doom. She felt her world shaking apart, sustained only by the arms clutching her.

She hated to need him. Especially after he'd asked to return to his previous, unfeeling, uncaring-about-Lillian state.

"You're not fine. Stop fighting me." He turned firm, as he'd been in the playroom two nights before. He adopted the Master persona that made her crumble and surrender to him during sex. As she was surrendering at that instant, though she hated to.

He picked her up and carried her to her bedroom. There, he stripped her naked and lay her on the bed. He joined her and spooned her from behind. He held her as she cried in fear and confusion, silent but comforting in his mere presence. Her Alek, steady and dependable as always. More than a means of support, no matter how she wished to refute it.

After a few minutes, she realized she was babbling. She had no idea how long she'd been doing so, in a steady stream of almost incoherent jabbering that gradually grew clearer.

"Don't go, don't erase the programs, I want you with me, I don't want the old Alek, I want you, please stay with me, please don't go…"

She had no idea how to shut off the flow of words as they poured forth. Throughout, he embraced her. He stroked her hair, her arm, her face, and occasionally shushed her…not as if he wished her to be quiet, but using the sound to comfort her.

Little by little, her moans tapered off. He soothed her, sheltered her. Reassurance crept over Lillian. She relaxed.

"I've got you. I won't go anywhere," He whispered in her ear.

For now or forever? She didn't dare ask. She was raw, her nerves too tender to withstand the slightest friction. She wept anew for a few minutes.

When she settled again, he shifted, moved away. She cried a wordless protest.

"Hush. I'm getting out of this suit, that's all. I'll stay right here, with you."

She subsided. She felt his movements at her back, then the heat of his naked skin against hers when he curled around her again. His arm slipped beneath her to clutch her beneath her breasts and hold her tight against himself, pinning her arms. The firmness of his erection against her ass was a welcome distraction, and she wriggled against it.

"That's it. I'm taking you where you can forget a little while. Where it's just you and me. Be my good girl, Lillian."

"Yes sir," she sighed and fell into the warm security of his control.

He cupped a breast, squeezed it, then played with her stiffening nipple. Darts of pleasure tingled when Alek wet his finger in her mouth and continued plucking the blushing tip. He smeared the wetness over her areola. A pinch started gently then increased until a jab of sensual hurt lanced from his touch. It sizzled an electric path to her cunt.

He toyed with her other breast in the same manner. He teased, squeezed, and pinched. She closed her eyes and sank into her role as his obedient slave, allowing him to do as he wished with her. She left behind her role as president of a multi-billion-dollar company that had come under deadly attack, left behind the responsibility, left behind those who plotted to harm her. She was a mere object of desire for her master, with nothing to offer but her docile compliance to his cravings.

His attentions moved from breast to breast, filling them with bliss and aching as his whims dictated. She moaned and trembled under his random impulses of tenderness and cruelty. She yielded to whatever was done to her. She delighted in it.

Alek stroked down her belly and homed in on where she was wet and already filled with longing. He stroked her clit, and she cried out at the jolt of rapture.

"Leg up on mine." He patted her thigh.

She lifted her upper leg off its twin and draped it over his. The position opened her to his thorough explorations. His fingers slid along her slit and delved deep between her pussy folds. He stroked the swelling lips of her labia, smearing more of her juices over her clit. It was difficult to remain still as he petted her, to keep her hips from rubbing her hungry cunt against his hand. To do so would have meant the bad punishment, however, where she'd be tied helpless, brought to the brink of orgasm over and over, but never allowed to come.

She lay quiescent, his for the taking.

Relief spread through Alek. Lillian's tears had ceased, though she continued to quiver. He hoped the tremors came from growing passion. With any luck, she was far from the emotional agonies of what had happened at CyberServe. She'd have to face up to them sooner or later, but for a little while, he could help her ride through the initial shock. He could give her the distance she required, so she could come back strong.

I'm not going anywhere.

For the immediate future, anyway. He had his own upheaval to work through. His matrix was warning to make no decisions about his programming on the heels of the explosion. He recognized he wasn't entirely rational, and the upswell of feeling for Lillian confounded his circuitry. He'd wait. He'd weigh his decision later, which had seemed so clear before.

In the present, he could indulge himself in what he wanted. In what she wanted. Alek could devote himself to her care and to his own desperation to be as close to her as possible.

He played with her clit and pussy and detected the tiny jerks of response as she fought to maintain her surrender to him. She was wet for him, eager for his use. He marveled that he was only now realizing the gift of her surrender, the joy of her trust in him, as far as it went. It was tempting to think he could throw caution to the wind and forge a forever bond. The mere idea brought warmth that redeemed all the uncomfortable emotions he'd experienced thus far.

Her breathing grew faster, until she was almost panting. She gave herself so easily when it came to sex. She trusted him when the clothes came off. Was there any chance she'd learn to trust him with more?

Later. When he had some distance from nearly losing her. When he could think logically.

He concentrated on the moment. He shifted her and put her in position for that first demanding thrust. She loved that instant of hurt-ecstasy that came from being taken all at once. He'd give her what she needed.

He obliged her desire by driving all the way in and exulted in her gasp as she was forced to yield. Her warmth grasped him, convulsed against him. Drew on him. Her pussy begged to be fucked with animal instinct.

He couldn't believe it hadn't occurred to him before to delight in joining with her as he presently did. The word *sacred* popped up in his processor. Yes, the connection they forged with their bodies was more than mere sexual coupling. It was a bond worthy of reverence. At long last, he understood.

Did he really wish to give up such a blessed union? Wasn't it worth the agony of the other feelings?

Again, he had to caution himself. *Wait. Wait.*

He wasn't sure he could.

Lillian moaned as Alek slid in her pussy, his movements slow but steady. He drew out the friction as his cock chafed against her inner hotspot. He caressed her clit, his fingers sliding over it, around and over. He made her quiver with electric zaps of sensation when he kept her pinned helpless and fucked her. He gave her existence meaning. He was her master, her savior.

He nibbled her ear and sucked the lobe. The attention increased the melting inside her. Such a funny little gesture to be so hot. But where their bodies came into contact, she went soft and compliant. Each move brought her closer to crescendo. He knew every inch of her, knew how to torment her. Knew how to bring her to screaming climax.

As if spurred by her thought, Alek thrust quicker, harder. Invading her again and again as he held her helpless. He didn't have to tie her down to make her defenseless. Didn't have to spank or discipline her to take her out of her own head. All it took was for him to hold her tight, to fuck her as he determined proper, and she caved into his strength. She felt each inch of his thick cock as it spread her open, as it speared deep within. He plucked and pinched her clit, and the excitement transformed into dizzying hunger.

Pounding her. Driving into her. The sparks flew, caught, grew. She combusted, an inferno awakening, shoving her over, pulling her under, yanking ecstasy from her. His cock jolted and joined her spasms as he filled her with hot passion.

"There's my girl," he whispered in her ear. He rubbed her clit to draw every last mote of bliss from her shaking body.

When he tried to withdraw, she reached to grab his ass, to hold him inside, though asserting her will could earn stern punishment. She couldn't help herself when she needed him so much. "Please."

"Just a change of position." He pulled out, rolled her onto her back, and shoved inside her once again. Her libido was shocked to renewed wakefulness at the abrupt invasion.

His weight pinned her to the mattress and held her hostage. His kiss was a tender counterpoint to the rough taking. He drew circles around her nipple with his thumb, and it sharpened to a point.

The kiss turned ruthless. His tongue plunged deep, seizing hers, forcing her to kiss him in return. The nerves in Lillian's body woke, shocked by the triple lightning bolts of his mouth feeding on hers, his hand squeezing her breast, his cock buried in her. Her insides quaked. She moaned and lost control for a thrilling instant, her legs curling to clutch at him. She froze.

He released the kiss and chuckled. "You may wrap your legs around me. Just to hang onto. Not to impose your will on me."

"Thank you, Master." Her calves settled against his muscled buttocks. The move lifted her groin and allowed him to push in deeper. She groaned as his crown crowded against something exquisitely sensitive inside.

He kissed her again, plundering, plunging, devouring until her thoughts ceased. His hips moved, drawing away slowly, until only the flared head of him remained inside. Then he drove in hard, and their bodies slapped together. His hot sack thudded against her ass.

Another slow withdrawal, followed by a demanding thrust that drove the breath out of her lungs.

"So fucking wet for me. So soft. So yielding." Slow withdrawal. "So eager to be rutted." Another breath-stealing lunge. He massaged his groin against her, abrading her clit, curling her insides.

He stroked, slow coming out, hard going in. He found her interior hotspot over and over. He ground against her clit. Lillian's pulse roared in her ears as lava filled her and threatened to erupt.

She panted, helpless beneath him, forced to concede to his strength. He stroked her breasts, the heat from his touch barreling straight to her cunt.

She tightened, the devouring hunger making her taut as she neared her end. Her cries were that of a small, trapped animal, unable to find escape. Closer with his every plunge. Closer with every grind of his hips. Closer with every pinch on her nipples. Closer. Closer…

Alek stopped moving slowly on the outswing. He pumped her hard, the friction unrelenting, and she fell apart. Destructive rapture rage through her, setting off violent spasms. Convulsions wracked her from head to toe. Another blast detonated when he released inside her, his cock jerking and warmth filling her.

"Lillian," he groaned. His kiss was gentle as the last convulsions faded. "What am I going to do with you?"

Lillian woke as morning's light warmed the fake windows of her room. Curled against naked flesh, but not Alek's chest or back. Her cheek pillowed against his thigh, and she snuggled against the rest of his leg. His hand rested on her shoulder.

He was sitting up against the tufted headrest of her bed. She was able to look at him without moving, without cluing him in on her wakefulness.

His sandy hair was rumpled despite its short style. His strong but angelic features were perfection, as always. What wasn't so perfect was the expression he wore. Doubt. Insecurity. His tawny eyes were unfocused as he stared at the wall across the room.

She guessed he was communing with his matrix. The learning portion of his processors were distinct from the main knowledge built into him and enhanced by the various programs he downloaded. Two different voices within him, informing each other at all times.

Going by the uncertainty she wasn't used to witnessing him display, she guessed he spoke to himself about her. What changes had the explosion at CyberServe wrought where his determination to break his emotional connection to her was concerned?

Don't go. The cry she'd spoken the night before reverberated in her head. She had her own two voices now. There was the experienced voice that said passions were too fickle. Even if he did something as insane as fall in love with her, that could change. He could find someone else.

The other voice insisted a relationship with Alek could be different. He'd seen her almost every day for the past year. Had listened to her, advised her at work, fucked her silly at home. He'd observed her at her temperamental worst. Watched her make bad decisions. With emotions encroaching on him, he still wanted to be with her. He craved her so much, it fucked with him and he had tried to run from it.

Lillian's feelings see-sawed as yearning and fear battled for supremacy. Alek was the first challenge she'd faced to her determination to remain aloof to love. She teetered, no longer certain she wished to go through life safe. Alone.

You have only today. Plan for the future, but do your best to live in the moment. Except for "I love you, my darling," those had been her mother's last words before succumbing to a virus she'd caught from a patient on Space Station Beta, when Lillian was thirteen.

Lillian very much desired to put her concerns to rest for a little while. She was horribly aware of how close she'd come to dying the evening before. How others *had* died, with no warning. What had they left undone in their lives? What would they have done differently if they'd realized they were down to their last hours of breath?

A fresh surge of terror swamped her. She couldn't open herself to heartbreak again. She couldn't give herself to someone and be lied to.

What if today was all she had left? If she knew that, how would Lillian live it?

She swallowed. Slowly sat up, her gaze riveted on Alek. The faraway look left his gaze as he turned to her.

Seconds later, they twined together. She cried out when he thrust deep and made them one.

Chapter Nine

"According to Detective Kahn, an explosive device had been attached to the shuttle of an executive assistant who worked on my floor. It's assumed the employee had no idea they brought the bomb in, since his body was among those retrieved from space." Lillian coughed to clear the catch in her throat.

On her home monitor, Tosha Cameron's and Brick's grim features reflected their sympathy. "What's the latest count?" Life Tech's CEO asked.

"Seventeen confirmed dead. Four remain missing." Lillian rushed from the harrowing subject. "Since the Freedom League was connected to the prior two incidents, law enforcement hauled Gunnar Jax in for questioning again. They're still interrogating him and a few other members of his lunatic fringe, but you know they'll get nothing. At least nothing on him."

"He's become a real thorn in our side," Brick growled. "I take it CyberServe remains in lockdown?"

"They've released all but the executive floor. That'll stay a crime scene for the foreseeable future. I have no idea when we'll be allowed to go in and clean up."

"Shut the whole company down for a week," Tosha said. "Tell your staff they'll be paid for the time off. I'll set up a crisis manager and psychological support for whomever needs it, for as long as they need it. Also, send me the names of the deceased as you suggested earlier. We'll do what we can for their families."

"Thank you, Mr. Cameron. I'm sure it'll be appreciated."

"Brick will look over CyberServe's security measures for an overhaul. I'm thinking the most state-of-the-art system. Beyond a mere upgrade, the best of the best, entirely new." Tosha was practically yelling in her passion. "We should have done that when the Freedom League first confronted you. No one should have died from my complacency."

"I don't think you've been complacent at all, Mr. Cameron." Lillian truly didn't. No one had carried out an attack on a company in the ITCS before. Business rivalry at its most extreme was dealt with by assassins, who took out their specific victims and few others. Terrorism was an Earth and outer frontier issue.

"Brick will take the lead, consult with industry leaders. We'll bring in your Mr. Michaels as a part of the team."

"If he doesn't quit. He took this latest blow personally. He's eaten up with guilt." The man had broken down and cried when Lillian spoke to him earlier that morning. She wondered if the gentle-natured security head hadn't gone into the wrong vocation.

"We'll talk with him, discover what we can do to keep him on. You're all right to return to work in a week? Or do you need longer?" Tosha showed care and concern.

"A week will be fine." She hoped.

After they broke the connection, Lillian turned to Alek, who had sat just out of the transmission feed in her living room, at a desk they'd set up for remote work. "Well, you heard the boss. We have nothing to do but sit tight for at least a week."

"I've already composed a text to the employees. I'm sending it now." He tapped on his keyboard. "Let's move on to your personal life. We should discuss your usual meet-up with your friends."

"I'll call them and tell them I'm a no-show." As much as she hated to give in to the terrorists, Lillian was too afraid to go to her usual lunch date. What if the Freedom League struck in a restaurant filled with innocent diners, killing Lillian's closest friends and people unconnected in any way with CyberServe? The guilt would destroy her, should she survive such an attack.

"I'm relieved you're choosing to stay in." Alek finished his tapping and set the keyboard aside. "Going out with this hanging over you would be a terrible idea."

"No kidding. As bad as it was to have CyberServe personnel murdered—" she choked on the word, swallowed, recovered "—they knew we were being targeted. Which doesn't make it any better, but for innocents to come under fire just because I'm out there…I can't."

"Let's invite your friends here. Security's beefed up throughout the building, the police are patrolling inside and outside the condo, and I'm here to keep an eye on you. Order a ton of food and booze from your favorite place. Have a party."

"Do you think it would be all right? We do have safeguards the level of a prison colony." Lillian wanted to say yes.

"I texted both Kahn and the condo security head earlier. They see no problem with you having your friends over. Inform the ladies how safe it'll be." Alek stroked her cheek. "It'll do you good to cut loose with them, if they don't mind the change in venue."

His eagerness to give her some semblance of normalcy warmed her through. "Thank you. I'll call them."

To Alek's relief, Lillian's friends were delighted to come to her condo and eager to lend their support to her after the explosion at CyberServe the day before.

"Jupiter's storm, I was frantic when I heard the news and couldn't get hold of you," black-haired Jenni said as she clutched Lillian in an enthusiastic hug. "What were the cops thinking, confiscating your phone for six hours? As if you'd blow up your own company and almost yourself!"

"Standard operating procedure," Phoebe said as she kissed Lillian on each cheek, her multitude of thin braids whispering against her silk shirt. Phoebe had studied law enforcement before switching to engineering. "Insurance fraud and conspiring with rival companies for a hefty payoff are always the go-to reasons for sabotage within an organization. Thank the stars and Sol you're okay."

Jody was a tearful mess under her electric-blue mohawk, her equally blue mascara running down her cheeks. "Bastards. What's wrong with those lunatic Terrans? I hope the courts space every last Freedom Leaguer."

Alek accepted their thanks for saving "their girl" and quickly poured the first round of wine. He'd met Lillian's crew in the past, since they'd often stopped by after work to lure her out for dancing. Once upon a time, they'd been four women and a man, the man being CyberServe's founder, Alexander Beauchamp. The engineering group had met in their jobs at an ITCS government think-tank, where Jenni, Phoebe, and Jody still worked. When Alexander had broken off and started CyberServe, Lillian had been the only one to follow him. She'd dared to leave the reliable paycheck and secure job she'd found stifling for the chance to bring about the next chapter of cyborg technology.

"One of us killed off by anti-cyborg fools is enough." Jenni fixed Lillian with a firm stare. "Don't you dare end up murdered like Alexander."

"Trust me, I'm doing my best."

Lillian appeared relieved when the conversation moved on to more pleasant subjects. Alek set out the trays of food that had been delivered and kept the engineers' glasses filled. He smiled at the laughter and easy banter that came from old friends who made it a point to stay close.

"This guy is amazing. I hope you realize the treasure you have in him." Phoebe gazed at Alek. "What about that rent-to-own plan, Lillian? I need a man about the house too, you know. Hey, how about a scratch-and-dent cyborg sale? You don't have to fix them all up so pretty. Let them go to us low-income gals at a discount."

More laughter. Lillian teased that no cyborg could handle Phoebe, and the rest agreed. The wine flowed and the women grew happier and louder. Lillian was flushed with drink and enjoyment. If her thoughts dwelled on her troubles with the Freedom League, she gave no sign. Alek was glad to see her relax.

The drunken lunch hadn't fixed everything, however. When Lillian took a long while to return from the bathroom, he abandoned his post at the dining table and Phoebe's increasing flirtations to check on her. From the hall, he heard Lillian's sobs in the bathroom.

He tapped on the door. "Lillian? Are you all right?"

She opened the door, wiping at her cheeks. Her eyes were red. Her breath hitched. When he put his arms around her, she pressed her hot face against his chest and bawled.

He pushed her into the bathroom and closed the door behind them so none of her friends would hear. He petted her hair, stroked her back, and uttered comforting noises. "Easy, now. I'm here. It's okay. What happened? What upset you?"

She moaned. "I upset me. I'm in there, drinking, laughing, having a grand time without a worry in the universe. Then I started thinking about the people who died yesterday. Their families. What kind of monster am I to carry on this way when they're sad and mourning?"

"You're no monster. You've been grieving. Didn't you call the next-of-kin this morning and cry with them? Put in a request to Tosha Cameron for their children to receive scholarships and dependent funding? You're doing well by those who were lost. It isn't wrong to try to be happy and enjoy your life between the moments of sadness."

She turned her face up to him. "It's not? Because I feel like I'm doing something wrong."

"You survived. That's worth celebrating." He kissed her, tasting the wine and the unnamable flavor that was all Lillian. "I certainly am."

She blinked and sniffled. "I guess so. I just feel so guilty. I'm in charge of CyberServe. If it weren't for me—"

"If it weren't for you, someone else would be dealing with the Freedom League. They might not have handled what's happened as well as you." He kissed her again. "You're doing fine, Lillian. Let's wash your face, put some drops in your eyes, and you can rejoin your friends."

He had her squared away, ready to return to the party, when she suddenly stopped and stared at him. She moved close. "Alek, I'm...you're...I mean..." she laughed self-consciously. "I'm drunk."

"A little. Which is why whatever you wish to say will wait until you aren't." He ignored the hopeful spark warming him. "Come on. The ladies are probably wondering where we disappeared to."

He'd no sooner gotten her to her chair when the doorbell rang. He answered it and carried a package through the great room.

"What's that?" Lillian called, once more laughing with her friends.

"A surprise. For later." He grinned and kept going toward the hall.

"I like surprises too, handsome," Phoebe called. A spate of laughter followed on his heels.

"You don't know the half of what he's capable of," Lillian cracked. "And I refuse to tell."

Shaking his head and chuckling, Alek took the container into the playroom. He unpacked its contents and set everything up for later, when he and Lillian were alone again.

On his return to the dining area, he paused at the end of the hall to listen to Jenni tell about a date she'd had the week before. The others laughed at her description of her hapless suitor's dancing, which had apparently been one part shaking and one part falling.

He concentrated on Lillian's tinkling giggles. Alek had never evaluated a person's laughter before, but he found himself doing so at that instant. The sound was...adorable. Yes, that was the word. Cute. Wonderful, like everything else about her. Even drunk and crying, she shone brighter than anyone else.

I was able to make her feel better. I enjoyed that.

He'd dried her tears. Convinced her smile. On a day that had started bleak, he'd brought in the friends she'd needed to dull the pain. He'd shown her that in the midst of shattering grief, joy could still be found.

He yearned to keep making her life better. It brought profound pleasure to him to be there for her. The emotions that came from doing so made him glad he'd gotten through their darker brothers of fear and jealousy.

If he felt the brighter sentiments more often than the others, it would be worthwhile to stay as he'd become. To love...he wouldn't mind if he could express that consistently, if he could continue to bring joy and comfort to Lillian.

I want that.

The big question was, could she learn to want it too? Could she overcome the heartache dealt in her past? Could she see him as more than a bodyguard? More than a cyborg sex partner?

The get-together lasted four hours. The moment Lillian's friends had to leave approached, and the three guests took their sobering pills and cleared their heads with the coffee Alek brewed. As they tested clean enough to safely pilot their shuttles, they drifted off. The flirtatious Phoebe, restored to a more temperate state, gave him her contact information.

"Message me tomorrow, and tell me how she's doing." She raked him with her dark gaze.

"I will. Thank you for coming. It meant a lot to her."

Lillian remained at the dining table. She drank her coffee and stared into its depths. Alek cleaned up the emptied food containers, wine bottles, and glasses.

She glanced up at him as his to-ing and fro-ing brought him near. The booze in her system nullified, she appeared ill at ease again. "Thanks for throwing such a great party. And for being there when I fell apart in the bathroom."

"Of course. I was glad you enjoyed yourself as much as you were able."

He carried out another load of post-party debris and let her brood. He refused to try to draw her out despite the sting of her withdrawing from him again. His matrix advised he let her work parts of it out, then it advised convincing her to talk about other matters.

Make up my mind, would you?

Analysis is difficult in terms of Lillian Kwolek's needs when she's upset. She has no specific pattern of verified solutions. This mood has been alleviated in the past by leaving her alone. It has also been made worse by leaving her alone. It has sometimes been eased by distraction. It has also led to her calling this unit an unfeeling computer when distraction is attempted.

She's human. Awfully, wonderfully human.

Please explain the contradictory descriptors used to evaluate her species.

Later.

Maybe. Probably not.

He returned to the dining area. "Your friends are wonderful to be so concerned about you. They jumped at the chance to be with you today. You're lucky."

That drew a smile. Distraction for the win.

"They're more than friends. They're family, especially after those years following my mother's death. I thought we'd grown a little apart since Alexander and I left the think tank where we all met, but yeah, they rushed right over today, didn't they?"

Alek sat next to her. "I'm glad they did. It seems humans do best with support."

"I suppose we do."

"May I ask something personal?"

"Since when do you wait for permission?" Lillian chuckled.

"I don't want you to think I'm being nosy. Unlike a few weeks ago, my interest is no longer purely focused on gathering data for my matrix."

She hesitated, then nodded. "Go ahead."

"You've told me about how close you were to your mother. How awful it was when she died while you were still young. What about your father?"

"Sperm donor."

"I figured. It's common enough."

"He was a topnotch engineer. Or is. Wouldn't it be funny if I've worked with him at some point and had no idea?"

Alek wondered if he should press for more information. He also wondered why he was so interested in her history, which had been a subject of only the barest curiosity before.

"You haven't remained in touch with whomever took you in after your mother's death, to my knowledge. Extended family?"

"Mom was an orphan herself. Her friends had no interest in raising a child. I went through two foster families before I was declared emancipated at sixteen. I went straight to college, then work."

"Why the second foster family?"

"The first had a son two years older than me. He got me drunk and took advantage. The household was labeled an 'inhospitable environment,' as the court put it. I was yanked out, put in therapy, paid a hefty restitution, and placed in a new foster home."

Alek winced. "And your foster brother received the mandatory lifetime monitoring sentence, I gather. Prison?"

"No, though he was found guilty. Because of his age, they went easy with a personality restructuring program. I understand he hasn't had a drink since and is the very pillar of his community on Luna Prime. The system worked in his case."

"In the end, perhaps, but that must have been traumatizing for you. The male animal hasn't been a great experience for you, has it? No wonder you don't trust them."

"Life's simpler without. But lonely," she admitted.

"Even with your friends."

"Even with them."

Alek could have kept pressing. He could have attempted to prove he was different from the men who'd harmed her. But he was on uncertain ground. It wasn't the right moment. Would he realize it when that instant arrived...if it ever arrived?

Chapter Ten

Lillian wanted nothing more than to drift into the security she felt with Alek. He was a man, at least superficially, but far from the inconsistent human male she feared. He was a cyborg with a matrix built on logic rather than foolish whims. Given time, the emotions that threw him so badly on occasion would gain more ascendance, but the rational computer core of him would remain.

He had no hidden agenda. No secret past, at least none since she'd activated him in CyberServe's research and development lab. Yes, under the command of Earth humans and the directives of his original matrix, he had an undoubtedly horrific history during the wars. But that had been another cyborg that no longer existed beyond its metal chassis. A creation long gone. A different entity altogether. Not Alek.

Was it possible to have an intimate relationship with whom he'd become? With the person he was becoming? Could she have love at long last, the kind of love that was built on unshakable trust?

Sentience had so many traps, however. Self-realization had more. It came with all the negatives that any human dealt with and too often fell prey to. Alek would find other women attractive. Maybe he already had. Later, he might decide to act on that attraction. He might find Lillian lacking and leave her for someone else. It was all too possible to be left hurting again.

She ached for more in her life so badly though. More than work. More than a few meetings with friends. She wished for that more to be with him.

"I wish I could keep you innocent," she burst out.

He stared at her, as if surprised. Then a grin she knew all too well twisted the corner of his mouth. "No, you don't."

She had to laugh despite her insides quivering with that excited, nervous, delicious churning. "We're talking about two different things."

"I know. You've had enough emotional upheavals for today, so I'm changing the subject. Let's do those impure, far-from-innocent acts we enjoy so much."

"Do they have anything to do with the package you brought in earlier?"

"They have everything to do with it." He stood and beckoned her to follow. "Come along, slave. Your master is eager to fuck you until his cum drips out of your holes."

As if she'd refuse an offer like that.

Lillian's questions and concerns about a real emotional attachment to Alek were suspended as she followed him to the playroom. Troubling matters began to fade from view as she shed her clothes outside the door. Upon entering that sensual space, worry disappeared entirely.

She gazed at the ropes hanging from the ceiling and the arrangement of black leather straps and silvery buckles suspended from the ropes. It was a harness, and her excitement rose at the thought of all the possibilities it offered.

So many straps! She couldn't quite make out how they were to be arranged, but she imagined she'd be wrapped as tight as when Alek had practiced shibari on her.

"We'll start with the usual exhibition of obedience to your master. To the spanking bench while I decide what form of discipline to use on you."

She fairly flew to the padded bench. She bent over it, her legs spread, her entire body quivering as she waited for him. She was already wet, and she imagined her pussy dripped its eagerness to the floor.

As much as she appreciated the spankings, she half-hoped it would be over quickly. She could hardly wait to see what would happen with the harness.

Alek's footfalls drew close. Lillian gripped the bench as he kneaded her ass, readying her for his discipline. Did it give him joy to spank her since his emotions had been sparked? She'd have to ask him later if he was getting anything out of it. Now that he could experience an emotional reaction, she needed to know what that reaction was.

Relax, she reminded herself as his massage ended. Her rear tingled from the rough caresses. It was time to attend to the present.

His first strike assured her there would be no problem on that score. A thick, heavy strap splatted across her ass cheeks, its end curling around her hip. Blazing hurt startled a yip from her.

"I heard that, slave. Extra lashes for your impertinent protest."

"Yes, Master. I'm sorry, Master."

He applied her punishment with a will and blistered her bottom to show his displeasure. She clung to the spanking bench with all her strength. By sheer force of will, she choked off the moans that battled to escape. It took every ounce of her eagerness to obey him to fight off the urge to flinch.

Three strikes in, he paused. His fingers slipped through her folds, and he found her wet. He shoved two digits within, and she quaked at the sudden invasion. Her greedy cunt pulled at him, eager for any kindness.

He withdrew and continued the spanking. Five harsh slaps from the strap scorched her ass before he broke off again. Once more, he cupped her crotch and pushed into her.

Finger-fucking her to send arousal soaring, to bring her close to climax before spanking her again.

Bit by bit, the violent pain transformed into thrilling warmth. The heat sank deep into her flesh. Her panting became gasps of pleasure as endorphins charged to her rescue. Desire heightened with each blow and doubled during the breaks when he plunged fingers inside her.

Whether he strapped her or plumbed her cunt, her mind chanted *I'm his, I'm his, I'm his…*

His. In those minutes, there was no doubt. Lillian belonged to Alek.

Her mind was fogged when the punishment ended. He slung the strap over the bench. "Are you grateful for this demonstration, slave?"

"Yes, Master. With all my heart, I thank you."

"Show me your gratitude that I give you my time and effort."

She slid to her knees and turned to him. His eager cock was already out of his pants. She crawled to him and kissed its length from tip to base. He allowed her to dote on him for several minutes before nudging her toward the corner where he'd hung the harness.

She crawled to it, though he hadn't told her to, eager to show her surrender. When she crouched beneath the harness, he showed her the leather cuffs. "Behind your back."

He put them on her and hooked them together. He also cuffed her ankles, but he didn't attach them to each other.

"Stand."

Lillian clambered to her feet, gratefully accepting his assistance. She was always so shaky after a spanking, especially when he played with her pussy as well. Her legs trembled as Alek began winding the straps around her torso.

Much as he'd done with the shibari rope, he trapped her breasts between leather bands to frame them. With an approving grunt, he spanked the mounds with his palms, darkening their color. She pressed her lips together to stop the cries that wanted to come from his stinging discipline. She locked her knees to keep from rubbing her thighs together in answer to the desire his rough attention brought boiling. He kissed the sting away and sucked her nipples hard so they swelled and jutted to his satisfaction.

He fastened more of the harness against her ribs, taking care so she wasn't bound too tight. Then he lifted her, her weight supported by one arm, and circled another belt about her waist.

She marveled at his strength. Not just that he could hold her up so easily, but that he had the sort of control that kept him from doing real damage when he spanked her. Was it any wonder she trusted him when it came to doling out the tormenting delights she adored? Why shouldn't she trust him with the rest?

He released her, and she hung from the straps and ropes, her torso horizontal. He worked on her ankles and thighs next. He bent her knees so her ankles nearly touched her ass. Her thighs were set wide, splaying her cunt for whatever he chose to do with it.

He slapped his palm once to each buttock to set off heady stings from the tender flesh. Another clap to her pussy made her jerk. He followed the pain with pleasure by mouthing her soaked folds until she shook violently under the assault. His tongue flicked her clit until she spasmed in warning.

Then he clipped her cuffed wrists to a strap depending from the ceiling and carefully tautened it, so her arms were raised as far as was comfortable. Lastly, he affixed a cup that cradled her chin and lifted it so she faced the wall.

He grasped a dangling rope and showed how it allowed him to raise and lower her to whatever height he wished. He locked it down when her face was on level with his.

"There's a well-bound slave, ready for her master to enjoy," Alek said, his gaze proprietary. "Give us a kiss with those sweet, plump lips."

Lillian sank into his possession by submitting to the tongue that explored and claimed hers. With her suspended as she was, he was free to fondle her breasts. He squeezed them until her breath quickened with mingled excitement and hurt. His thumbs played with her nipples, goading the stiff points to grow harder. He kissed and caressed until she was dizzy with bliss.

Her lips tingled when he released her, tender from his demanding use. He grasped the rope and lowered her to the level of his waiting cock. "Now for the best kiss of all."

His hand on the suspending straps rocked her. He brought her open mouth to his waiting shaft. His flesh rubbed over her tongue, back and forth. She closed her lips on him and firmed the grip for his delight. His hips moved to greet her as she swung close. The motion sent his crown into her throat.

His to fuck deep, whether it was her mouth, pussy, or ass. Lillian fell into the rapture of existing to serve him however he deemed right. She swallowed and gagged on the pulsing length he fed her, her devotion to him growing with every thrust. With each demand, she fell deeper under his spell.

"Every drop I give you," he commanded. "Don't let any spill."

When had she ever? But it always felt good to be given an order she'd obey without hesitation.

Alek's eyes rolled, and he groaned as he let go. Salty-sweet warmth filled her mouth, and she swallowed what he gave her, her cunt flexing its wish to be treated to the same.

Afterward, he stood there and let her lick him worshipfully. He patted her cheek. "Well done. I'm ready to enjoy that hot, wet pussy."

He walked around to her splayed sex. Lillian was tugged upward, so she floated high over the floor. Did that mean…?

She bit her lips together as his tongue delved into her. No sound without permission. Their play was her fantasy that her needs were less than his, that she existed for his pleasure alone. For Alek to give her what she wanted…what she *needed*…he'd have to punish her for daring to assume he wished to hear her enjoyment.

She kept as quiet as her increasing respiration allowed, her eyes screwed closed as he licked, kissed, stabbed into her. As he occasionally lapped and sucked her clit. He feasted on her quivering pussy, eating her out with a proficiency she was certain no sex star could claim.

"Would you like to come?" he asked as she trembled and fought her body's demand that she do so.

"If my master wishes it of me," she gasped.

"Hm." He filled her with his finger. He found the exquisite spot within and rubbed. She almost lost control then and there. Her pussy clutched hard. "I don't wish to spoil my slave. But there is something satisfying about a servant who'll come on command. It is your highest priority to obey me, isn't it?"

"Always, Master," she sobbed, hanging on by the thinnest thread as the friction lit an inferno.

"Then climax. Now." He licked her clit.

Blinding whiteness filled her vision. The first surge barreled through her, a cannon blast through her senses. It was far from the last. He continued to pump her pussy, and he sucked her clit as well. He drew scream after scream from her as orgasm rampaged in continuous heaves.

When she was at last depleted, shaking and sobbing in the aftermath, he patted her sex affectionately. "Such enthusiastic compliance. I'm pleased with you. What do you say?"

"Thank you, Master."

"You're welcome. I'll fill this well-trained cunt with my cock, and you may display your joy to serve me as often as you wish."

He lowered her toward the floor. To groin level. Lillian had barely an instant to register the pressure on her pussy before he thrust all the way into her swollen passage. His groin clapped against her ass.

It was as if the invasion pushed the breath from her lungs. Her mouth gaped wide, but she was unable to scream without oxygen. Resounding hurt somehow twisted itself into ecstasy, and orgasm engulfed her.

Somehow, she heard Alek over the roaring in her ears. "That's it, tight little cunt. Milk my cock. Yes."

Air whooped into her chest as she relearned how to inhale. Ragged cries burst from her as his steady strokes woke multiple surges of powerful bliss. She quaked in the creaking harness as he swung her to meet his every thrust. His thick cock rubbed unerringly over her internal hotspot and prolonged the elation.

When her shaking frame attempted to quiet, he reached beneath to stroke her clit and set her off again. "Keep coming for me, slave. I love the feeling of your hungry cunt squeezing me, begging me to keep fucking it."

He wouldn't let up, and she couldn't stop him. Orgasm swiftly became as much torment as reward, spending tension only to have it build again. How many times did he force climax on her? She lost track as he kept her on the knife's edge of brutal rapture.

She couldn't even find the ability to beg for mercy as he shattered her again and again. The unending enthrallment of his thickness driving deep, his educated fingers toying with excruciating perfection on her clit, his absolute power over her, and her inability to defend herself in any way…it all combined to leave her the victim to his unsparing attention.

Only when he had her utterly wrecked did he allow himself climax. He grunted like an animal with each jet of cum. When he went still, Lillian sagged in the harness. Her sobs were weak, her body trembling.

Alek patted her ass as he pulled loose. "Be right back. I'm going to grab a vibrator for the next round.

She would have wept harder, but she didn't have the strength. How would she survive more of his attentions?

He gave her little opportunity to formulate a protest that wouldn't end with punishment. He made sure she saw the small pad that he wore ringed on the ends of two fingers. The vibrator was tiny, but she knew from experience it was powerful. Her pussy clenched as if it could somehow protect her clit, which throbbed from too much attention.

He stood behind her again. He gripped her strapped buttocks and held her in place as his cockhead nestled against her snugger hole. She almost moaned a protest, but stopped herself in time. She had no choice.

The knowledge brought a fresh swell of heat to her lower parts. At such times, she wished she'd been equipped with an off-switch. Her libido was ridiculous.

Alek pressed into her, still wet from the deep dive into her pussy juices. He'd not stretched her, and her ass yielded grudgingly. She panted against the growing ache, inwardly cursing herself as her pussy flexed in eagerness at the harsh use. Mingled excitement and hurt swirled in a heady brew, ignoring how often and how hard she'd already come.

Pain slut. Bondage whore. Nymphomaniac. She was all those and more. He knew exactly how to use those qualities against her.

"Feel that thick cock invading your ass. Making you take every fat inch of me. You'll come while I use your tight hole, while I fill it with cum. You love it when I take you this way, in this filthy, debased manner."

She shook under the physical and verbal assault, unable to deny the truth. He probably didn't need to use the vibrator to make her climax, either.

Her shaking increased when he stroked her pussy. "Just as I thought. Wet; wetter than when I fucked it. Damned near dripping."

His groin tucked to her ass. He'd sheathed his entirety in her, filling her to bursting. Her mind swam with endorphins, brought on by excitement, pain, and orgasm. He was still playing with her slit, rubbing her pussy lips and waking the maelstrom.

He drew out halfway, then slid in again. At the same instant, the vibrator hummed to life, and he settled it against her clit.

He chuckled over her tiny cries as her insides twisted. "That's it. That's what gets you off. That's what you *love*."

As she adjusted to his girth, he rutted her harder and faster. All the while, he kept the thrumming pad pressed hard to her clit. It sent waves of carnal hunger through her. There was nothing but that demanding rubbing within and the demanding throbbing without. Her focus narrowed to the sensations of ass and clit, with all else falling away: the harness, the room, the rest of her, even Alek himself.

Ecstasy seared her. Ribbons of extreme pleasure unfurled, rolling thick and heavy and sweet inside. Lillian dissolved in blinding brilliance and mighty pulses.

She returned to quieting waves of rapture and the jolts of his shaft as it filled her with warmth that overflowed, trickling to the floor beneath her. His sighs sang in her ears.

"Jupiter's storm, that's beautiful, my cum leaking from your ass. I saved half the sack just to see this. It was fucking worth it."

A smile drifted over her lips at his enthusiasm. Fucking worth it, indeed. In that moment when she was too euphoric to pretend, she decided a great deal of her life had been fucking worth the bullshit to arrive at that moment.

Chapter Eleven

The week passed with life's typical waves of ups and downs. Lillian did her best to get as much work completed from home as possible. What she could accomplish was the drudge labor of reading and writing reports, meeting over video channels with department heads and the executive board, and reviewing analyses from CyberServe's various divisions. What she couldn't accomplish was the fun part of her position: sneaking into R & D to develop new programs, showing cyborgs to prospective buyers, or keep deliveries of sold cyborgs on schedule since all of CyberServe was closed.

Half a dozen employees quit, so her managers were scrambling to fill positions. Two customers canceled their cyborg orders. The remains of eighteen people were recovered, with only a few bits of DNA detected from the remaining missing, who were declared dead.

Not all the news was bad, however. By the end of the week, the cops finished the evidence-gathering portion of their work, releasing CyberServe so its employees could return to the undamaged portion of its headquarters. Brick and Mr. Michaels conferred with the president of Alpha Security Consultants, the leading security specialists of Alpha Space Station. The instant the police released CyberServe to its owner, repair crews and the security company swooped in to fix and refit. Some of the techs, though they'd been granted the entire week off with pay, rushed to their labs as well. Lillian could understand. She itched to go to CyberServe, not to play her part as president, but to goof off in the labs. If Alek hadn't pointed out the latest security measures weren't at full capacity yet, she would have.

Her boss was adamant on that point too.

"It's only for a few more days. Brick and Mr. Michaels are confident CyberServe will be well guarded from here on out," Tosha assured Lillian during their video meeting. "Everything is being checked several times over to keep you and your employees safe. The Freedom League maniacs won't get a toe in from now on."

After touching base with Michaels and the security company's president, Lillian felt confident too. Only military and government installations had more safeguards than CyberServe would enjoy.

Work life promised to return to normal. Home life was even better.

Lillian was far from having slogged through her fears where emotional investment was concerned. She admitted she had fallen in love with Alek, and was reasonably sure if he wasn't in love with her too, he was on the verge. She confessed that only to herself. When she imagined committing to a true relationship, a hot, sick ball formed in her gut. She wasn't ready, but she took heart in the notion she was inching closer with every happy second that passed.

She was blissful with anticipation of the day she'd be able to tell him the truth of her feelings. The sex, with devotion added, was the best it had ever been. Waking up in his arms, his smile greeting her the instant she opened her eyes, was sheer heaven. Even the hours spent while they worked in her living space, exchanging only business-related information, took on a specialness.

Her future was full of the promise she'd avoided hoping for in the aftermath of the last heartbreak. With each passing moment, Lillian believed happily ever after was possible after all.

"Ugh, where is that file? Damn it." Lillian cursed at her computer, which refused to cough up the information she required for her meeting taking place at CyberServe in three days. Had she erased it by accident?

No worries. Alek would have it on his system. Trouble was, he'd ducked into the shower, and Lillian being Lillian, she wanted it at that instant.

"Demanding instant gratification should be among the deadly sins," she sighed, disgruntled with her own impatience. Nevertheless, she stood up from the sofa and crossed the living room to the chair and small table Alek had set up as a home office. She tapped through his files and sighed again at how wonderfully organized he was. It wasn't the first time she'd noted how much quicker she could find what she needed on his computer rather than her own.

"There you are," she said less than a minute later. "Alek, you're the best."

She opened his mail server to send the file to herself, with the mental warning to save it where she'd be able to find it from now on. She went as far as to write a note in the body of the message: *don't be a dope. Put this where I can find it, damn it.*

Chuckling, she delivered it to her mail.

Alek had his server set up to list mailed messages whenever a new one was sent out. Her gaze fell on a familiar address as the record appeared: Ingeniumphoebeum.sec2as.

She frowned. Why would Alek be messaging Phoebe?

The screen below the entry was a hodgepodge of message entries, most to CyberServe's various departments. Scattered among them was Phoebe's address on multiple lines. One or two a day. Sometimes more.

Lillian scrolled down, her heart thumping slow but loud. She found the first of the many mails, transmitted a few days before. The morning after Phoebe and her other friends had come for that drunken lunch.

Feeling sick, Lillian clicked on the message. And read.

Hello again, Phoebe.

Yes, it was wonderful to have you here. You certainly brightened the place up after our close call yesterday. No, I don't believe you behaved foolishly at all. Your warm, smiling presence was a delight.

As for your invitation to drop by, I'm flattered. I'd like to—

The sound of Alek's footsteps in the hall, heading for the living room, brought a rush of panic. Lillian hurriedly closed the message, then snarled a curse at herself for doing so. What did she have to feel guilty about? Why did she feel she'd done something wrong when Alek…when he…

Bastard.

He stepped into the room, his hair damp, freshly scrubbed face shining. He stopped short when he saw her at his computer. "Hey. What are you…no, let me guess. Did you lose the security clearances file?"

She stood up. She pointed at his computer, trying to steady her shaking hand. "What is going on between you and Phoebe?"

Alek's smile froze. Guilt made it vanish. The shame on his face exposed all she needed to know.

She'd been duped. Again.

He gathered himself and squared his shoulders. "Look, I can't help she won't get the message I'm not interested. I thought about being downright rude, but as you said, she's your friend. It makes me sick inside to think you'd have to choose between me and someone you regard as family."

"She came on to you?"

"You read her messages, right? And mine? If you saw the last one, from yesterday, you noted I told her I wouldn't respond to any further mails."

Some of the pain dulled. He had turned Phoebe down for whatever she'd suggested. Remembering how her friend had touched and flirted with him, Lillian could easily gather what Phoebe had wanted.

Maybe she'd supposed Lillian wouldn't mind since Alek was a cyborg. To most humans, the former war machines were things, no matter how sentient they appeared. Neither the monsters Terrans saw them as, nor the living, emotional beings people such as Lillian and Tosha had learned they could become. It hurt that Phoebe would message Alek behind Lillian's back, but it was possible she saw it as no more consequential than borrowing an outfit.

Then why didn't she ask you if she could borrow him?

Lillian shoved the question of Phoebe aside. It was Alek's secretiveness she had to deal with, the clandestine way he'd conducted himself. It wasn't as horrid a betrayal as she'd initially believed, but it was a betrayal nonetheless.

"Why did you hide this from me? You should have told me she put you in an awkward position."

He looked trapped, reminding her of her married lover's reaction when she'd shown up at his home, when she and his wife had confronted him about his duplicity. The memory heightened her anger and sense of betrayal.

She was in no mood for the excuses that poured from him. "I had no idea what to do. My matrix gave me conflicting options. It warned you might blame me for being the reason Phoebe behaved as she did. I did my best to avoid leading her on, but you might have believed it was my fault. You might have…have hated me. After you told me how much your friends meant to you, how Phoebe was family…I was afraid you might be upset."

"You thought I *might* be upset? Knowing my history with men, my distrust of men?"

"That was the biggest reason I was afraid to tell you. I worried you wouldn't trust me." He held his hands out in helpless supplication. "I was terrified of losing you. I love you, Lillian."

Her guts twisted with nausea. She'd known an Alek with emotions could learn to be deceitful, but she hadn't expected it to happen so soon. "Have you not heard anything I've said to you? How could you not realize I needed the truth, no matter how painful? How could you miss that anything less than absolute honesty would destroy every ounce of faith I have in you?"

He stared at her with a look that said he'd been punched in the gut. Good. It was about time someone knew how it felt to have their faith trampled all over. To be lied to about what mattered more than anything else. To have their heart ripped out and stomped.

"I'm sorry," he said. "I never meant to…Lillian…"

"You have to leave."

The desperate suffering that filled his expression was a knife to her heart. But she had to have space to ponder the situation. Time for her outrage to settle, so she wasn't allowing past hurts to color her feelings about the blow she'd been dealt.

"Lillian, don't. Please."

She returned to her computer and typed out a message for one of the techs at CyberServe. "I'm having another cyborg loaded with the security software and flown over. As soon as it arrives, you can return to your berth at CyberServe."

"Lillian—"

"This isn't open to discussion, Alek. I have nothing else to say to you." She left him standing there, the agony they shared stamped on his features.

She stormed to her bedroom and locked the door. Then she crumpled on her bed and muffled her sobs in her pillow.

Chapter Twelve

Alek blinked at the huge figure who let him into CyberServe's security wing.

"Hi, Alek. I'm surprised to see you here. Is Lillian with you?" Brick stared at the shuttle bay behind Alek, where he'd left the vessel his replacement had flown to Lillian's home.

His replacement. It made his circuits churn, though he found some relief that a female Infiltrator model had been sent in his stead. He doubted Lillian had any intention of intimacies with a female cyborg. She wasn't built for same-sex frolics, as so many humans were.

His relief was miniscule, however. He'd lost far more than a sex partner less than an hour before.

"Lillian no longer wants my services as a bodyguard." Or anything else. His world was shattered.

Brick must have discerned some of it, because he winced. "I'm sorry to hear it, Alek. You've been excellent in that capacity. Come on in. Mind the mess."

The corridor among the security offices wasn't so much a mess as crowded. Machinery, probes, detection devices, scanners, and more lined the walls. Alek studied a pile of tangled black straps, next to several rows of shoes. It looked as if a herd of squid had tied itself in knots.

Noticing his confusion, Brick explained, "Tethers. Some of the work has to be done outside the station. Suction boots and tethers are used to keep the installation crew from having to use booster packs, unless they somehow drift off and need to fly back."

"Ah. Where is the crew?"

"Lunch break. Come on; we can go in the office. Tell me what happened with Lillian."

Alek wasn't sure he should share personal information, but Brick had evolved enough to enjoy a meaningful, committed relationship with Tosha. Maybe they'd had problems too, outside of assassins continuously trying to kill Life Tech's CEO.

They settled in chairs on the guest side of Mr. Michaels' desk in his office. Alek's gaze was drawn to the monitors that showed the damaged executive section. Construction tools, looking as if they'd been laid down minutes before, scattered the floors. Wiring and conduits hung from the exposed ceilings. Apparently, that crew had gone on break as well. "The new bulkhead's in place. Still looks like a long way to go before it's ready for use."

"CyberServe will be operating without that level for a week before you can move in. The other two levels that were damaged are already finished." Brick leaned toward him, his broad features exhibiting friendly concern with perfect human characteristics. "So. You and Lillian. A fight? Was it bad?"

"I messed up. I blurted out that I loved her, and that made it worse. She ordered me to leave." Crushing despair, which he'd somehow held the worst of at bay until that moment, overwhelmed Alek. "It's over before it really began. Everything I was afraid of…it's here. It's happened."

"That's awful." Brick's sympathy failed to take the pain away, but something in Alek appreciated it. It was good to be heard.

"Did things ever go bad between you and Tosha like this?"

"Not within our relationship."

"So you don't know how this feels. You can't relate to living in fear that the worst will happen, then it does. Which is good. I wouldn't wish this on even Gunnar Jax."

Brick shook his head. "I didn't say I had no understanding of losing Tosha. I went through hell where that was concerned. Still do, when she gets a death threat from the maniacs who have nothing better to do than terrorize those in the public eye. I'm happy for the most part, but I'm also terrified I'll lose her."

"It's awful. I hate having feelings."

"Probably because you're hurting right now. When things are going well, it's worth it."

Alek remembered having moments when he'd felt that way. Those moments had been fleeting. "I don't think the tradeoff for a minute or two...or even a night...compensates for this. Especially since Lillian is finished with me."

As Brick grimaced with commiseration, Alek sank into his loss in all its awfulness. Lillian no longer wanted him. He had nothing left. Literally, nothing.

Brick made no request for him to help with any of the ongoing security installation, and Alek didn't offer. Instead, he trudged to his old berth where he'd spent off hours when he wasn't working or staying with Lillian.

He glanced at other off-duty cyborgs in the assistants' chamber, standing in their cocoon glass enclosures, powered down until they were activated for their shifts. Most of them worked in the labs, assisting engineers and researchers. A few were like him, aides to executives.

Would Lillian trade him for a different assistant? His announcement he loved her would make for an uncomfortable environment for both of them. Not to mention the fact he'd betrayed her trust. She'd most assuredly swap him out for another.

He sat at a computer bank in the middle of the chamber, provided for the cyborgs who worked at CyberServe. They used the computer for education and betterment when they weren't on duty. Without certain programs, they lacked the natural curiosity of humans, but their matrixes were geared to learn. In the course of their days, they often came across situations and questions that produced the urge to acquire more knowledge.

Alek remembered his life before he'd acquired emotions. Had it really been only weeks ago? Before then, he'd occasionally experienced dim pleasure to have successfully acquitted his duties as Lillian's assistant. And a quieter gratification to sit at a computer bank and feed his matrix the information it wished to gather. There'd been none of the harsh tug-of-war between agony and ecstasy. That had come as he'd developed too many feelings.

Emotions. Passionate sensations. The incredible highs always seemed to be followed by crushing lows. Brick was wrong. It wasn't worth it.

It was clear to Alek he'd have been better off to have never developed sentiment of any sort. Now that he had, it was time to start fresh, from scratch.

A whole different life. Since Alek was owned by CyberServe, it would be up to Lillian to agree to it. No doubt she would. She wouldn't want a lovesick cyborg around...and he had no wish to be around either.

It was the only sensible path. He was too emotionally corrupted to be sold to a buyer. His sole option was to cut his current existence off and forge forward to the next.

In the midst of his unabated misery, he found a measure of hope. He'd hit upon the answer. It was a relief within the awful grief that accompanied the idea of losing Lillian. No, not the idea. The reality. There was no going back.

Alek switched on the computer he sat at. Typed what was necessary for his first step toward freedom. Then he went to his old berth, stepped in, and deactivated himself without a reactivation setting.

MINE TO KEEP

* * * *

Three days after Lillian had sent Alek away, two hours before CyberServe officially re-opened from its weeklong hiatus, she docked in the showroom level's bay, where temporary offices for the executives had been set up. She glanced at the cyborg who'd taken on the duty as her bodyguard in the interim.

"Step out and do your sweep. I need a few minutes to think."

"As you wish, Mr. Kwolek," the SIF responded in her purring tone. The tall, elegant Infiltrator stood and left the vessel.

A few minutes to think? How much more thinking did she require? She'd had three shitty days and even shittier nights during which she'd barely slept a wink.

She'd been wrong to send Alek away. She understood that now. In the devastation of the moment when she'd learned he'd been secretly communicating with Phoebe, the overriding urge to be free of him and the hurt he'd represented had been overwhelming. With everything she'd feared since realizing how much he'd come to mean to her coming true, her only goal had been to crawl into her bed, lick her wounds, and swear off romance yet again.

Her bruised ego had refused to acknowledge Alek's basic innocence in the matter. Yes, he'd failed to tell her about Phoebe's attempts to seduce him...attempts he'd refused time and again, as she had discovered when she read the mails on the computer he'd left behind. She'd recognized his growing desperation behind the polite responses that offered excuse after excuse to refuse Phoebe.

Lillian knew him and his thoughts, even in the wake of his new emotional gains. She had buried herself in engineering and programming the cyborgs too deeply to not understand Alek perhaps better than he understood himself. Not to mention the hours she'd spent with him day in and day out. She'd watched him grow and develop like a child within her household.

She'd let her fears and wounded pride separate them. He'd extended his love, and she'd ignored it. No, she'd done worse than that. She'd thrown his love aside. Because she grasped how he operated, she was all too aware he'd never have spoken the words unless he meant them.

He loved her. And she'd ordered him to leave.

She had struggled with what to do during their separation. There was no doubt of her first move: she had to apologize to Alek. She had to ask him to forgive her for her callous rejection, for her inability to see beyond her own past wounds to his present ones. Her confusion lay in what came next.

Did she tell him she loved him too? Everything within her quailed at the prospect of opening herself up to potential trouble in the future. She'd lost her shit over a situation that hadn't been his fault. What if he did eventually turn to someone else? How awful would such a loss be then?

Could she stand to lose him now, when there was a chance at the happiness she'd given up on...a real, honest-to-Jupiter chance at long-lasting love? How insane would that be? Sure, she'd be protecting herself from a cataclysmic loss...but the glorious future with Alek she'd be sacrificing at the altar of safety was akin to refusing a trillion dollars for fear of someone stealing it later.

Lillian rubbed her forehead, where the worst ache throbbed. She appreciated what any intelligent, strong woman would do in her shoes. But if she fucked up again as she had three days prior, she'd hurt Alek. Maybe as badly as she'd been damaged. He didn't deserve a relationship with a woman who flew off the handle and punished him for the sins of the men who'd come before. He deserved better than the mess she was.

Apologize. Come clean with all that stands in our way. Then discover what happens next.

It wasn't a clear path, but it was the best she could come up with. With a sigh, she got out of the pilot's chair and left the shuttle.

She went to the temporary office that had been set up for her, in what was typically a room where clients could interview prospective cyborgs and test out any programs they'd had implemented on those already purchased. As the SIF took up a guard position in the doorway, Lillian hurried into the small space where a couple of scrounged desks and chairs had been squeezed in between couches, a bar, and tables.

Alek wasn't there.

"Greetings, Mr. Kwolek." Alek's recorded voice emitted from hidden speakers. "You have a message waiting from your executive assistant Alek. Should I play it?"

Lillian frowned at the formal tone, but some of her anxiety eased to hear his voice. "Yes, go ahead."

"Hello, Mr. Kwolek. I trust you are well since our parting. Having given careful consideration to our last verbal exchange, I tender an official request to have all my programs removed and my matrix wiped clean. I feel I can no longer serve in any helpful capacity to CyberServe—"

"Damn it!" she shouted over his voice. She dropped her computer bag on the floor and hurried to the door. "You cold, robotic bastard, I'll—"

Since she had no idea what she'd do, she stopped threatening. Instead, Lillian rushed to the corridor with the silent SIF trotting after her.

Chapter Thirteen

The SIF's presence irritated her, but that was easily rectified. "Go to your berth after I reach Alek. Your services as my bodyguard are no longer required," Lillian snarled.

"Understood. The assistant PSM called Alek will resume the responsibility," the cyborg said in her seductive voice.

Damned straight he would.

Lillian charged into the standby chamber. She ignored the SIF as it stepped into its cocoon and shut down. Her gaze found Alek, unaware in his own berth, his eyes closed, chin tilted toward his chest, as if he'd fallen asleep standing. Which was essentially what he'd done.

She jabbed the button on the berth's controls to command his matrix to power him up again. Fists clenched at her sides, she watched as his head swung erect, as his eyes opened.

"Alek online." Awareness flooded his expression, and he gazed at her. His jaw tightened.

She ignored the sick feeling that rose at his obvious tension at her presence. She raged instead. "A matrix wipe? It took you a year to achieve all you have. All you are. And you want to erase it?"

"Yes."

When he said nothing more, she snapped. "That's great, Alek. That's the logical choice. We've had a tiff, so you decide to wipe out everything you've become. A sort of suicide. Do you not understand how irrational your request is?"

He stepped out of his berth, his facial muscles twitching. Stony impassiveness was replaced by torment, then anger. Actual anger, though his tone remained level.

"A tiff? As in a squabble? A spat? A slight disagreement? Is that how you'd define throwing me out of your life?"

Was that how he'd taken it? She'd had no intention to call it quits entirely. "I didn't. I needed space. Time to think. To deal with…" *my bruised ego*, her mind finished. She cleared her throat and started again. "Look, you recognize where my psyche is after my previous relationships. Especially that last one. How you go from 'give me a few days to figure this out' to erasing your matrix is ludicrous."

"Is it?"

"You know it is!"

"Let's see what I've learned from you," Alek retorted. Fury simmered under his composed words. "Relationships go bad. Therefore, all relationships are to be avoided. We shouldn't even talk about them, except under the influence of alcohol. Essentially, they are to be deleted from existence, both past and future."

She blinked at him. "But…but that's not right at all."

"You plan to have a romantic connection in the future?"

She struggled with confusion. "I thought maybe…if you and I could..." A stab of fear thrust into her heart. "I mean, I care about you, but I'm scared."

"What about Phoebe?"

"Phoebe?" Her bewilderment increased. "I'm done with her. Based on the messages she sent you, she knew how underhanded her behavior was. Our friendship is over."

"That's your typical response to someone who's injured you."

"In Phoebe's case, it's beyond hurt. It's betrayal."

"What exactly are your parameters for betrayal?"

Lillian gaped. "I…well…"

"You don't know. Yet with little thought or consideration, you've removed her from your life. She no longer exists, as far as you're concerned, though you described her to me as family."

Lillian scowled. "She didn't act like family. She deceived me."

"You erase those who betray you." Before she could protest, he added, "Tell me an occasion when you haven't."

She gaped at him. And realized she couldn't. Since the married lover incident, she'd only needed a whiff of deception, and a relationship was ended. Friends, her foster families…including the one that had and hadn't raised a sexual predator. Anyone.

Alek let sadness peek through. "As I told you, I've fallen in love with you. Sooner or later, whether or not I mean to, I'll screw up again. It's human nature…or in my case, self-realized sentient nature. You say you weren't cutting me out of your life when you sent me here, but you were. You've second-guessed that decision, which is a good sign. But you'll do it again. Maybe then, you'll mean it."

"I don't want you to reboot. You matter too much to me." It was the only argument she could come up with, though her mind worked frantically to discover an argument against what he said.

He smiled. "I like hearing that. But unless you can do more, it's best to forget the whole thing."

"It's not. Alec, wiping your matrix isn't the answer. It can't be."

"You live in your past, and I can't exist wondering when your trauma will destroy the only reason I have to remain self-aware. I can't live this way. Especially if it means I'll end up without you."

Tell him you love him. The truth is the only hope to fix this. Tell him!

The words stuck in her throat. He wasn't the only one terrified of being tossed aside. He had no idea how awful it was to love someone with everything in his soul only to find out it was a lie.

"I can do better. I will do better. I just need time."

"I can't take that chance. I want a complete system reboot. It's the only answer." His firm tone wavered. "Please, Lillian. I need out. It's what you would do."

"No, I wouldn't. Damn it, just stop!"

Before he could argue any further, she spun and ran out. She escaped to her temporary office.

Hiding. Running away. After all, as Alek had said, it was what she did over and over.

She closed the door behind her. She leaned against it, trembling and wondering what the hell she was supposed to do.

Lose Alek? Everything in her screamed against it. He couldn't wipe his matrix. It would kill her.

Then you'll have to tell him you love him. She'd have to open herself to a committed relationship and maybe lose him in the end. She'd have to put herself on the line if she wanted to keep him.

That felt equally impossible. She'd sworn she'd never be that vulnerable again.

Lillian groaned. How was she supposed to decide?

She noted the balcony outside the room, a small bubble outside the office. It looked out on the stars. She pushed herself off the door and headed for it.

She stood on the platform, and her gaze drifted over the star-studded blanket of the eternal night. The thing about being a space station-dwelling starkid was there were often such places to go and stare at the cosmos. It reminded a person that however overwhelming his or her problems might appear, next to the universe, it was all trivial.

People fell into two camps: those who felt their lack of worth against the immensity of the infinite, and those who found calm and freedom when they realized nothing they could do would destroy it. Lillian tended to fall within the second camp. The endless starscape reassured her that however big her problems appeared to be, they were miniscule in the larger scheme of things. It gave her perspective.

Her mind settled and calmed. The panic nipping at her ceased. Anxiety still churned in her gut, but it no longer overwhelmed her. She could think again.

Okay, so try to be objective. Look at the situation from the big picture angle. What do you see?

She saw Lillian, a woman who'd suffered loss and disappointment. She'd had to pick herself up and brush herself off after being knocked down on multiple occasions. She'd not only survived all that had happened to her, but had thrived in many areas of her life. She'd become the successful engineer she'd wanted to be. She'd helped create an entire company. She'd been advanced to head up that company.

The personal happiness category was where she'd come up short. Relationships had come and most had gone. Her trust had been put in the wrong people on occasion, leading her to lose faith in love. To set it aside. Hell, to lock her heart in a box to gather dust.

Now, there was Alek. He loved her. She loved him. The choice was to try to make it work, at the risk of being heartbroken yet again. Or to remain safe from a disappointment that might never come.

Lillian frowned. She hadn't thought of it in those terms before. For years, it had felt as if the outcome of any potential relationship was destined for destruction. After discovering the truth of her married lover, she'd forgotten the chance of any other possible result.

She could have love. It didn't have to fall apart with Alek.

It might. She couldn't deny that. But it might not.

For the first instant in years, she allowed herself to imagine things working out. To visualize months…years…a lifetime…with Alek. She envisioned him never leaving her for another. Or leaving at all.

Was it possible?

Of course it was. People had such relationships. Her friend Jody had been married for the last fifteen years, and the relationship showed no signs of falling apart. Many of her co-workers were also in committed partnerships that had stretched into decades.

I thought I could have that before, and it went to hell.

It had. But her first affair had been when she was barely out of her teens. Truth be told, she couldn't imagine still being with that guy, even if he hadn't cheated on her. She could chalk up the bastard who'd hidden his marriage from her up to bad luck. After all, she was the only one among her acquaintances, at least that she was aware of, who'd experienced such an awful situation.

Alek loved her. He loved her so much, he preferred to have his matrix start from scratch than live with the memory of what little they'd had. He'd asked to be erased to avoid mourning the life they could have but wouldn't.

Lillian swiped at the tears tickling her cheeks. Their relationship might go bad. But it also might go well. She had a chance with Alek. She'd be a fool to refuse it.

Don't let two assholes keep you from the perfect man. Don't let them take more than what they already have. Alek is worth the risk.

"Now all I have to do is convince him how I feel. Woof, that'll be another level of debate, won't it?" she asked herself.

She drew a deep breath. Now that she'd made her decision, the old anxieties woke again and demanded to know if she really wanted to expose herself to the worst that could happen.

For anyone else, no. For Alek...

"Absolutely."

She blew a kiss to the lightyears of stars and space before her, thanking them for yet again clarifying her perceptions. She turned, left the balcony, and headed for the door.

She hurried to find Alek, instead of running from him.

She was halfway across the room, a hopeful smile creeping out, when the door opened. At least a dozen people swarmed in, Gunnar Jax leading the group.

"What—what are you doing here?" Lillian halted in shock before the staring group. "How did you get in here?"

Jax laughed, his smile bright within his unkempt beard as he and his followers paused. "Hey, here's the cyber slut all by her lonesome. Shouldn't have ditched your bodyguards, Kwolek. My Freedom League has members working in all the ITCS's security teams. Including CyberServe, Life Tech, and Alpha Security Consultants." He nodded at a woman in a CyberServe security uniform who looked vaguely familiar to Lillian.

As he boasted, she glanced around for something to defend herself with. Unfortunately, the room's function as either a meeting lounge or temporary office offered nothing in the way of weaponry. Especially when there were so many.

The group moved around her. "We got the big dog. Cyber Slut herself. See? I'm more than a figurehead." Jax nudged bushy-haired Artemis Neera, who stood beside him.

Her return smile was tightlipped but indulgent. Her glare for Lillian burned with raw hatred, however. "You did good, Gunnar. Let's take care of business."

She caressed the handle of a knife, sheathed at her hip, with one hand. With the other, she hefted a gun, the sort Lillian had seen only in Earth movies. Neera stepped close to her and pointed the barrel inches from her face.

Chapter Fourteen

The Freedom League terrorists marched Lillian through the still-empty halls. The workday wasn't scheduled to begin for over an hour more, so it wasn't startling to see little evidence of staff. However, security should have been assembled outside her office door, warned of the Freedom League's presence by the surveillance cameras posted at regular intervals. Was the entire department compromised, including Michaels? Or had the Freedom League taken them all captive...or worse, killed them? Lillian hoped it was a matter of the monitors being offline, that the security force was unharmed and simply unaware she'd been attacked.

As she was escorted through CyberServe, she considered telling her captors that a single weapon pointed at her was enough. In addition to Neera's antique firearm, nearly everyone had leveled a weapon of some sort at her. Some had gren-guns, which would literally blow her to pieces if they shot her.

They weren't ready to kill her yet. They needed her for something, though they hadn't told her what. She could guess their objective, due to her surroundings and the direction they marched her in.

She swallowed and followed Jax. She did her best to avoid thinking about the ten or so muzzles aimed at her from behind and on either side. She possessed little knowledge about weapons, other than one pulled a trigger and bad things happened on the other end. She'd watched enough dramas to have learned that sometimes firearms went off by accident. Somebody got too nervous or too excited, or the device malfunctioned and fired. People got hurt when that happened.

It was on the tip of her tongue to point that out. That maybe whoever was the best-trained with weaponry should be the only person allowed to guard her. She wouldn't be much good to them if she were dead.

The Freedom League was no doubt aware there were others who would make good hostages. Others who knew how to operate CyberServe's various systems. Lillian had a suspicion that the curdling hatred coming from Neera wouldn't require a whole lot of encouragement to ignite an explosion. Lillian was expendable when it came right down to it, and Neera might be more than happy to prove that point.

She kept her mouth shut and hoped no one, whether accidentally or on purpose, would kill her. Because if she spoke up, a *mistake* was more likely to happen.

Just as she'd suspected they would, Jax and his goons took her to CyberServe's largest storage bay.

For a few seconds, Jax's group gaped at the rows upon rows of cyborgs within the vast space. Humanlike bodies stood at attention, both on the floor and suspended five columns in the air, held in place by magnetic rails. It was the largest bank of CyberServe's inventory, five hundred thousand units, all awaiting repairs and upgrades. Two-thirds were still operational in some capacity, despite the damage they'd suffered in the war. Even nude, as most of them were, they were an impressive sight.

"Shit," someone groaned. "It's my worst nightmares come to life."

"Fuck this," another said in a panicked voice, his pulse rifle pointing first at one group of insensible cyborgs, then another. "Let's get out of here."

"They're powered down," Jax soothed despite eyeing his surroundings with obvious fear. "They're about to be made so they'll never operate again. Be cool."

"Secure the area," Neera ordered the woman wearing the CyberServe security uniform and holding a gren-gun. Those two had been the only members of the group who'd kept their weapons targeted on Lillian.

The officer turned to the door they'd come through and punched commands into its manual control panel. "Got it. No one can access the bay from here. I'll barricade the other three doors." She took off.

"All right, cyber slut." Neera waved her gun in Lillian's face. "Over to the computer bank. Now."

She did as she was told. She walked to the massive workstation, where the monitors were all dark. What did they expect her to do with half a million cyborgs?

"Switch it on." Neera's heavy brows descended low over her eyes, as if she'd expected Lillian to already be working on whatever plan the Freedom League had concocted. "But don't power up those garbage cans. If any cyborg so much as twitches, I'll blow your brains out."

Lillian cocked her head as her finger hovered over a computer's *on* switch. "There's no power to the station."

The next instant, she stared at the floor, which had appeared only a foot from her nose. Her ears rang a strident tone. She blinked to find herself stretched on the ground, propped on her elbows. How had she ended up there?

Pain blasted through her head an instant later. She cried out and grabbed just behind her ear. A lump was already swelling.

"Stand up, bitch. Wake this fucking thing up." Standing over her, Neera snarled and brandished her gun.

Jax grinned over her shoulder. "That's telling her, babe. Hey, here's the power." He jabbed the switch and frowned when nothing happened. "She's right. It's got no juice."

"I want it on *now*!" Neera shrieked.

Lillian looked down the long, black barrel of the gun. She licked her lips, but her tongue was as dry as a desert. "It was probably shut down at the main source while the place was locked down. Let me check."

She hauled herself up, shaking her head to clear it from the blow Neera had dealt. *She must have hit me with the gun's grip.*

The muzzle dug into her cheek. "Stop delaying! Move it, cunt!"

"I'm going."

As Lillian dragged herself around the workstation to where the power module was, she reflected on the situation. Neera was unhinged. It seemed that the rumors about the Freedom League had been true: crazy as she was, she was in charge, not Gunnar Jax. He was merely the poster boy of the organization. The "figurehead," as he'd put it.

The computer station's main power grid had been taken offline. Lillian switched it on. Though the computers themselves remained inert, a hum announced the energy source had been restored.

"Get a computer running. Hurry up." Neera sounded breathless with excitement, her eyes alight with hectic eagerness.

Lillian went to the first available station and turned it on. The welcome screen invited her to enter her passcode. With Neera tapping her skull impatiently with the gun's barrel, she did so.

"Okay, it's up and running."

"Good. Set the cyborgs for self-destruct."

Lillian turned to stare at her. She did her best to ignore the deadly bore of the gun's muzzle in her face. "What? Like, wipe their matrixes? Because they don't have the same matrixes they did on Earth. They've been outfitted with—"

"Blow them up, bitch!" Neera sprayed her with spittle as she screeched. "Make them self-destruct. Explode the whole bunch."

Lillian gaped open-mouthed. "They don't have explosives attached to them. That would be insane."

She cringed against the computer station as Neera raised the gun with the obvious intent to bash her skull with it again.

The extremist's expression flickered with a note of sanity as Jax grabbed her arm to stop her. "Hold up. Let me try," he coaxed Neera. He offered Lillian a charming smile. "You need to cooperate, or I can't guarantee you'll come out of this alive. Look, we've seen the how it works in the movies. The rogue ship or robot always has a self-destruct failsafe that blows it up."

Lillian would have laughed at his naivety if her life hadn't been hanging by a thread. Did Jax and Neera actually believe real life was accurately represented in films? Had their home planet fallen so far behind that Terrans believed movies were on the level of documentaries?

She supposed they might. Earth had once been the hub of human ingenuity, until the corporations had funneled all technological breakthroughs into fighting territorial wars for resources. The engineers and scientists, at least those who could escape, did so to the ITCS's string of space stations. After the rebels had stopped the corporations and wrested control from them, there'd been few technicians left. With their world in shambles, a massive lack of infrastructure, and depleted resources, Terrans had been left scrounging just to keep the lights on.

Could members of the Freedom League have been reduced to thinking the height of engineering and technology was represented in Earth's old movies and television shows?

"Listen," Lillian said as Neera wavered. "The cyborgs you're looking at have been wiped of all programming. A number of these don't have any operational function whatsoever. Those that do aren't capable of anything more than following basic orders. Walk. Talk. Stand still. Make me a drink. Clean the toilet. That sort of thing. The barest of tasks. What they were on Earth is gone. Erased."

"You lie. I've seen them work on their own. Laughing and acting without orders." Neera's fury was waking again.

"What you've witnessed are a few purchased cyborgs programmed with sophisticated interpersonal programs, chosen and tweaked by their owners." Lillian thought it best to avoid telling them the cyborgs were expanding into sentience and self-identity through those programs and the learning matrix.

Hell, she was fine with outright lying to the fanatics. "Really, they're only sophisticated toys in their current state. They're made to simulate our emotions for their owners' comfort."

"What if their owners are monsters? Do you vet your customers for that?" Neera grabbed Lillian by the hair. She dragged her to a row of worse-for-wear PSMs, the same model as Alek. "Do you know what these sophisticated *toys* did to me while I was in prison? I can't have children because of what happened!"

As she screamed at Lillian, she jerked her back and forth by the hair, tearing some of it out. Lillian gritted her teeth against the pain.

"There are safeguards in place to keep them from harming others that way. Even as bodyguards, they're programmed to defend only as much as it takes to keep their owners safe. It's hardwired into their circuits," she sobbed when Neera stopped yanking her around.

"Bitch, you have an answer for everything. You damned sure better come up with an answer on how to destroy them here and now, because otherwise, you're dead." Neera shoved the gun between her eyes.

Alarms began braying in the bay.

Chapter Fifteen

"Alek here."

"Man, am I glad you picked up." Michaels sounded out of breath. "When I didn't see you with the president, I was afraid…listen, Alek, the Freedom League's got Mr. Kwolek. I've called the police, but I'm scared they won't arrive in time to deal with this."

Alek bolted upright from the chair he'd been sagging in, at the computer mainframe in the cyborg cocoon bay. How had he missed hearing the alarms in the distance? How could he have been so absorbed in his sadness? "What do you mean, they have Lillian? Where is she?"

"Main storage bay. There's over a dozen of those lunatics in there with her, including Gunnar Jax and his girlfriend Neera. We only just saw them because the security cameras went down all over the site, and we had no one—"

"Feed me the monitors here," Alek interrupted. "Show me what's going on."

His circuits fired in a frenzy as the picture came up on the screens before him. Lillian cringed as Artemis Neera screamed obscenities while pulling her around by the hair. The extremist shoved her into a chair and waved an old revolver. Jax and others stood around. Some scowled at Lillian, and some watched the unpowered cyborgs that surrounded them.

It took all Alek had to keep from running straight to the storage bay and beating his way through the door with his fists. A strange, guttural noise rose, and after a second, he realized it came from him. A restrained scream seeped between his teeth.

Lillian waited for the verbal and physical assault to stop before saying, "The best I can do is access the mainframe and show you there's nothing I can do to destroy the cyborgs from here."

"We need to break in there and help her," Alek told Michaels. "First, let me take care of something."

"They have the bay locked up tight. One of my people, Mays...damn it, I checked her history with a fine-tooth comb. I did that with all of them! But she's in there too."

"Concentrate, Mr. Michaels. Order your squads to those doors and stand by. I have an idea."

"They're already there, trying to force their way in. What are you up to?"

"Following their playbook and getting help on the inside. Stand by. Come on, Lillian, let go and put some distance between you and the computer."

As if hearing him, she drew back and waved at the monitor, exhibiting terrified frustration as she glared at Neera. "See? These are all the commands available through the mainframe."

Neera shoved her aside. Jax joined his compatriot, shoving too. Lillian was nearly knocked out of her chair. She pushed away to let them look. Good. She had no contact with the keyboard whatsoever.

Alek disabled Lillian's passcode. Though he couldn't view her monitor through Neera and Jax, he knew it had begun flashing *Access Denied* when the pair shouted. They turned to confront Lillian.

Alek froze. "Leave her alone, assholes. You know she did nothing. Don't you fucking touch her."

Neera's gun came up, and he readied to reinstate Lillian's access before she was killed.

"What the fuck is this shit?" Neera shrieked.

Lillian held her hands up. "Security must have noticed I signed on. The alarms tell you they've been alerted you're in here with me. They've deleted me from the system."

It was Jax, of all people, who tried to talk Neera down. "Okay, so we're still cool. We have an important hostage. We use her to either hack into the system or to convince someone else to obliterate these monsters. No problem."

Neera looked as if she'd take the shot anyway, and Alek's fingers flew over his keyboard. He had access to the mainframe, and he inputted commands as fast as he could type.

His screen flashed *enable?* He hesitated and watched the drama within the bay, his finger poised over the command.

The set of Neera's shoulders loosened. Her brows, nearly meeting over the bridge of her nose, drew apart. "Yeah. Yeah, let's get someone on the horn, tell them our demands." She told Lillian, "You sit there. Don't move. Don't say anything."

Alek allowed his own tension to lessen the slightest bit. He tapped the keyboard, and *15:00* appeared on the monitors. It began to count down.

"Did you hear all that?" he asked Michaels.

"Every word. I expect it might be me they call."

"Stall them and be ready for things to go down in fifteen minutes. I'm on my way."

* * * *

Alek sped to the security level, conversed briefly with Michaels, then raced to the level below where Lillian was being held. Seconds later, he stepped out of an airlock.

He'd decided against the precious minutes necessary to pull on a full spacesuit. Gloves, shoes, and a collar to which he could seal his helmet were all the protection he'd afforded his lab-grown collagen dermis. He was relying heavily on his circuitry and systems to regulate his temperature in the hopes most of his skin wouldn't be too badly damaged during his climb up the outside of CyberServe's hull.

He used a single tether rope that he attached to the maintenance rungs as he went. The suction shoes and gloves kept him clinging to the station like a fly on a wall.

He climbed. By the time he reached the storage level of the company, almost a minute had elapsed. His sensors sent warnings that fluid vaporization had begun in his unprotected skin. He was also slowly freezing. Ironically, with the sun beaming its rays and without an atmosphere to protect him, he'd possibly end up with a nasty sunburn where his skin was exposed.

His circuitry worked frantically to offset damage, but Alek wasn't concerned. Even if his entire dermal covering was torn off, which there was no danger of, his matrix and processors were safely enclosed within his metal chassis.

He let the matrix complain without heeding it. His only thought was to reach Lillian.

He left the vertical climb to approach the main storage bay laterally. Meanwhile, the timer continued to count. He eyed the distance between him and the airlock attached to the bay. He'd underestimated how long it would take him to make the journey, but there was nothing he could do about that.

He continued to crawl to Lillian. He learned as he went that a cyborg could pray when it came to the saving of the woman he loved.

* * * *

Lillian kept the same attention on Neera she'd have given a short-circuiting industrial robotic meat cleaver. Though the Freedom League appeared to have the advantage, what with a high-value hostage in their clutches, the situation hadn't gone according to plan. The latest snafu was in convincing Mr. Michaels to do what they wished.

"I don't have clearance to activate the cyborgs, so I don't have a passcode into that system," Michaels insisted over the communications link.

"I don't want them activated for the hundredth time. I want them destroyed!" Neera pounded on the computer station with her fist, purple from frustration.

"I don't have the ability to do that either."

"Then who does? Look, you're begging me to start sending you pieces of your boss—"

"If you could just give me a chance to contact a member of the engineering staff. They're the ones who understand how the cyborgs work. Or you could wait for them to show up for work in about half an hour—"

Jax snorted and glanced at Lillian, his expression almost sympathetic. "Damn, does he have it out for you? I'd swear he wants Artemis to start carving you up. Or is it a case of little to pick from as far as employees goes? Hey, Alison. You work for the guy. Is he dumb?"

The security guard with the nametag Mays on her chest shrugged. "Michaels never struck me as stupid. Overworked and stressed, sure. He always looks like he's at the end of his rope. Maybe this is what finally does it for him."

Or he's buying time. The thought gave Lillian hope he was stalling until law enforcement showed up. But then what? She would still be used by Neera as a pawn.

"You guys, shut up," Neera snarled. She returned her attention to Michaels' voice. "Someone has to do something about these fucking machines *now*."

"You've always avoided being caught before. They'll know you were a part of this," Lillian dared to whisper to Jax.

His easy grin assumed a reverential aspect. "This is the blow that needs to be landed. Wiping out the cyborgs, erasing them from existence, will make us heroes on Earth. It'll heal the wounds Terrans carry. It'll give us closure. We need that more than anything, including our freedom. I'll go to prison with a clear conscience."

"Didn't you find closure from executing some of those responsible for the corporations that carried out the wars?"

"A little, yeah. But those bastards were faceless, for the most part. The cyborgs…that's what we saw every day. What we fought every day. Their destruction will right the wrongs we suffered."

He spoke with zealot's fanaticism, even with his voice reduced to a mutter. That Gunnar Jax believed in what he said was obvious. Added to Neera's trauma and hatred of cyborgs, it was clear Lillian wouldn't leave the bay alive. She represented everything they were against.

Before that could happen, however, she decided to learn what she could. "Why didn't you bring explosives yourselves? Why not do to the bay what you did to the executive level?"

He gave her a derisive smirk. "We couldn't bring a lot of ordinance from Earth. You must have heard how hard the ITCS makes it to sneak the materials through. It's next to impossible to get half of what we needed on your black market too. That tiny explosion represented all we could get our hands on. It barely took out a quarter of your office's floor, far less than what it would take to demolish even the smallest storage unit of your cyborgs."

Lillian hadn't realized any of that, but she wasn't in the market of smuggling contraband into the ITCS either. It granted her a small measure of relief that the ITCS was so vigilant.

Neera broke off her conversation with Michaels. "What a useless piece of shit. He says he'll have an engineer contact us as soon as one arrives. I gave him five minutes."

"Don't let him delay beyond that. The police are probably here," Mays scowled. She kept her weapon pointed at the cyborgs with the most threatening appearances, the TWMs and TWFs. Many of the others did as well.

"Let's have some fun while we wait." Gunnar's excitement was a bizarre counterpoint to their dark moods. "A few of us have weapons that will demolish the tin cans. We can start the party without the destruct codes."

"No distractions," Neera ordered. "We aren't here to destroy a few dozen. They're all scrap."

"Yeah, of course, but it'd be a gas to personally trash a few instead of letting a computer have all the glory. Think of the pictures we could circulate to our supporters—"

A hum rang through the air. The Freedom League jolted to startled attention, their gazes skittered everywhere. "What's going on?" Mays shouted.

"If that ass Michaels is playing a trick, you'll pay for it," Neera cried, shoving her gun in Lillian's face again.

A scream rang out, then another. Neera's aim jerked aside as she reacted to the horrified cries of her people.

Thousands of cyborgs opened their eyes. Most of the units' visual sensors, stripped of colored lenses, glowed a hellish orange. Pinpoints of tangerine-colored light filled the chamber, as if a swarm of fireflies had woken all at once.

Lillian took her opportunity and dropped to the floor. She crab-scuttled to hide beneath the computer station.

"Kill them!" someone—she thought it was Jax—shouted.

A bedlam of firing from different weapons exploded in Lillian's ears. She clapped her palms to them, barely making out the thuds of hundreds of feet as the rows of cyborgs standing on the floor began to march.

The cyborgs were unarmed, but they could withstand a great deal of abuse before succumbing. Only the gren-guns would take them down after several shots, and Lillian had counted no more than half a dozen of those wielded by her captors.

It had taken decades for the Terrans to overcome the cyborgs and throw aside the control of their corporate masters. A couple dozen poorly armed insurgents wouldn't stop even naked cyborgs from doing whatever someone had ordered them to do. Not when there were so many.

"Shit!" Jax screamed. The lone unarmed member of the group, he ran a few steps in one direction, then another, and another. "Shit! Let me outta here!"

Lillian wasn't sticking around to watch the cyborgs overcome the Freedom League. She crawled under the computer station's desk surface overhang to put distance between her and her captors, Neera in particular.

She crept behind her assailants' legs and neared the corner of the long computer bank. She noted how the front lines of the approaching cyborgs fell as those with the right guns fired on them. Yet the cyborgs continued to come, with the TWMs and TWFs—the Walls—leading the charge. How long could the Freedom League hold out against them?

Lillian reached the corner of the computer bank, and a pair of boots ran to cut her off. Neera knelt on the floor, her features a mask of unholy hatred as she pointed her ancient gun at Lillian.

Chapter Sixteen

Alek pulled the airlock's door shut behind himself. All over his torso, arms, and legs, he could feel the damage the frozen space had done without his matrix reciting it to him. It didn't matter.

He heard weapons firing in the bay beyond the airlock, but there was no possibility of forcing his way into the storage bay until the chamber he inhabited finished pressurizing. A full minute, during which anything could happen to Lillian.

Or had already happened. The cyborgs would have activated two minutes before. Had the Freedom League killed her immediately? Or were they continuing to use her to hold off the automatons he'd ordered to keep Lillian from harm, to rescue her if possible?

Alek's matrix had offered damned little hope of keeping her alive. It identified what was already certain: whether she got what she wanted or not, Neera would kill Lillian. His only recourse had been to provide a distraction and possibly save her. He'd soon find out if he'd managed to do so, or if he'd accelerated her death.

He bared his teeth at the airlock door. *Open, damn it.*

* * * *

Behind the line of Freedom League radicals, Lillian yelped as Neera dragged her out from under the mainframe by her hair. "Deactivate them! Make them stop, or so help me, I'll kill you!"

"I. Don't. Have. Control. Over. Them!" Lillian enunciated every word, though she held little hope Neera would listen in her present state of panic. She'd refused to acknowledge a word Lillian had said when she had control over the situation. The chances of her accepting the truth of the situation during full-scale battle were nil.

"Artemis! Artemis! You have to get me out of here!" Jax ran wildly back and forth, hunching to hide at the back of the firing line.

"Not without killing this bitch and taking out as many of them as possible," Neera snarled.

Lillian had run out of time. It was in the crazed shine of Neera's dark eyes, wide enough to show the whites around her irises. She was ready to murder her.

Lillian yanked to the side, ignoring the brutal tug of Neera's grip on the silver locks. At the same instant, she shoved against her attacker's wrist and the hand holding the gun.

It went off. Her ear, next to it but just out of the line of fire, lost all its hearing. Ignoring how close she'd come to having a bullet in her brain, she lowered her head and butted it hard into Neera's chest.

Neera exhaled in a gust of explosive air and fell flat on her ass. Gripping Lillian's hair, she pulled her down as well. Lillian crashed on top of her. The gun was jarred loose and slid across the floor off a couple feet, out of reach.

They fought each other, swinging and kicking. Pain registered from the blows, but Lillian's survival instinct had been triggered, and she gave Neera everything she had. They paused pounding on each other to scramble for the gun when they had the opportunity to lunge. Neera screeched at the still-panicking Jax. "Help me with her!"

He paused long enough to shout, "Fuck you! You got us into this!"

Lillian jerked loose and brushed her fingertips on the gun only to have Neera slam her skull to the floor. She saw stars and lost her tenuous hold. Neera sprang for the weapon as Jax, taking advantage of a gap that appeared between the encroaching cyborgs, made a beeline for the door that led to an airlock.

"Bastard! Coward! *Traitor*!" Neera brought the gun up and fired several shots…into Jax's back. He stumbled forward a few steps, then fell. He lay unmoving.

Lillian saw it from her position, flattened to the floor. The crazed energy that had fed her combat with Neera had fled. Only sheer will forced her past the ringing in her head so she could bring herself to her hands and knees. The knowledge that Neera would turn and kill her too brought her up on shaking legs.

Perhaps that would have been the case, had the airlock door Jax had been running for not chosen that instant to open. Alek, wearing a space helmet, stepped out. He sighted Lillian beyond Neera and ran straight for them.

Neera screamed as the PSM shot toward her, a ululating cry of a child trapped in a nightmare. "Not you! Not *you*! Kill it! Kill it!"

She fired a barrage at Alek. The bullets couldn't have gone through his metal chassis, but Mays, alerted by her leader's hysterical screams, turned the more powerful gren-gun on the approaching cyborg and fired too.

Alek went down in a hail of explosive shots, his shirt and flesh shredding. The metal beneath was pocked with holes.

"Alek!" Lillian shoved past the still-screaming Neera, whose gun clicked impotently as she continued to shoot from an empty chamber. Lillian tackled Mays to the ground. The next few seconds were a senseless, chaotic blur. She was aware she was punching Mays, who lay under her. A distant voice in her mind howled for her to look out for the other woman's weapon, but her body was far from lucid control. Its only goal was to keep her foe from destroying Alek.

"Mr. Kwolek! Mr. Kwolek!"

Hands tore her from the bloodied Mays. A man whom Lillian didn't recognize right away replaced the view.

"Mr. Kwolek, we're here. We have them contained."

A woman joined him. "Mr. Kwolek. Lillian? Are you okay?"

"Officer...Kahn? Mr. Michaels?" Her brain began to reassert itself and overcome desperate instinct.

"Hey, there you are. Are you injured? Yeah, scalp's bleeding, and you're going to have a hell of a shiner. How many fingers do you see?" Kahn held up three.

Lillian was far from interested in counting fingers. She shot from security, cops, and cyborgs gone motionless to the only person who mattered. "Alek!"

He lay prone, the white fluid that fed and nourished his skin soaking his torn shirt and tie. He stared sightlessly at the ceiling.

Power re-routing. Partial functionality will be restored in five seconds. Four. Three. Two. One.

A face hovered over him. Human. Female. Wetness ran down her cheeks. More wetness, red in color, from her scalp.

"Partial functionality restored."

"Alek, thank the heavens. Are you okay? How do you feel?"

Feeding pertinent information to vocal emitters.

"This unit is attempting to regain its functions after a sudden, unplanned shutdown. Systems are rerouting paths to undamaged circuits. Some systems may be permanently lost."

"Your memory, Alek. Do you remember me?"

Human is referring to this unit as Alek *instead of its serial designation. Respond to her questions.*

"Negative. Memory circuits appear to have experienced catastrophic feedback from explosive injury to main network. Please stand by for further data."

More wetness, pouring heavier from her eyes. Her voice grated, choked. The PSM...he knew that was his designation, though the human female kept calling him *Alek*...felt a tugging at his chest.

"Give me a light, someone. I have to see how bad he was hit."

A beam flashed bright against his visual sensors, then trained onto his torso. The female grimaced.

"Damn it. There's damage to your main power supply. It must have sent a surge into your matrix. Most of the CPU is apparently functional since you're talking, but...*fuck*. If any engineers have shown up, bring them!"

The PSM felt something. A strange urge to learn the reason for the odd play of facial tics she displayed. But no, only performing the tasks required of it mattered. "The current matrix is heavily damaged. The most economically and labor-feasible solution would be for a new matrix to replace the impaired piece. Shall this unit power down for the repair?"

She made odd noises that weren't speech. Harsh, hiccupping sounds to go along with the flow of wetness. *Tears*.

"I don't want you to have a new matrix. We may not be able to transfer your memories and feelings to another one. We have to fix this module. Have to." She slapped her hands over her face, the bizarre sounds growing louder. "I can't lose you. I have to get you back. Alek, come back to me."

Lillian bawled, her sobs growing in violence. She didn't care that she was surrounded by law enforcement and CyberServe's security. She never had cared what others thought of her preference for cyborgs when it came to her personal life. Now that she had actual feelings for a nonhuman, she gave zero fucks what they thought of that either. Especially when it came to the opinions of the Freedom League, cuffed in the middle of the room. Most particularly she gave absolutely no fucks about Artemis Neera, who'd killed her boyfriend, who kept shouting *cyber slut* until Detective Steelman threatened to have her sedated.

None of that mattered when Alek didn't know Lillian. Compared to that, everything else was a blip on her radar.

It was to be expected. Gren bullets were explosive, and though Alek's matrix hadn't been impacted dead-on, it had suffered harm. The question was, how much was too much?

She inspected the damage, recalled the importance of the various circuits that had been impacted. Data storage appeared mostly intact, but its housing was crumpled on one edge and a quarter of the neural pathways feeding to it were inoperative. Too many to know without a schematic how badly the device had been compromised.

Maybe the matrix could recover his memories. Perhaps even his feelings for her, little as he wanted them. If it failed to, repairing it might restore everything. Maybe.

She was forced to count a lot on a possibility that might turn out to be unfeasible. So Lillian cried unashamed tears and begged Alek to return.

He'd loved her. She'd been too stupid to appreciate that and what it had cost him. Too determined to never be hurt again to accept his precious gift. She'd squandered it all. There'd been a few days she could have lived the perfect relationship with the man who'd offered her everything. She'd missed out on it because she couldn't stand to tell him those three little words that would have meant the universe to him.

He'd suffered the version of a cyborg death in coming to rescue her. He'd done so despite believing she didn't care for him. Despite her treating him worse than those who'd lied to her. Infinitely worse. Without his memories, she'd never be able to make it up to Alek.

"Lillian?"

Her hands flung to either side, though she hardly dared to believe Alek had spoken her name.

He gazed up at her, the bland lack of feeling giving way to confusion and a hint of desperation as he sought to regain what he'd known.

"Lillian?"

He remembered her name. He remembered being around her. In an office. In a home.

"Alek?" She looked terrified. Why was she scared?

"Stand by. Records of interactions are coming online."

More stored data arrived. A memory of her standing over him, leaning down to look over his shoulder at a computer screen. Another in which she typed on her own keyboard, writing lines of programs. Cyborg programs. Programs for her to test on him.

A vision of her naked before him, approaching with her head bowed. Of her kneeling before him...

...of her urgently sucking his cock into her mouth. Her warm, wet mouth...

...lying beneath him. He pinned her, taking her with force, but her expression said it was what she wanted, what she needed...

...and feelings. Emotions. Too many emotions crowding in faster than his matrix could cope with. Terror rose in him that matched the expression she wore as she leaned over him, still crying. An aching need to be with her, to protect her. Adoration, as pure and light as a star but also heavy and hurtful, because…because…

"Do you know me? Do you remember?" She cried harder and cupped his jaw. "Alek, please. You have to return, so I can tell you I'm sorry. So I can tell you I love you. Alek…"

The maelstrom eased. Pieces, not all but most, fell into place. Illuminated by three words, his world, atilt in a sea of blank spaces and shattered edges, began to right itself.

I love you.

"Lillian. Lillian." He reached for her and pulled her down for a kiss. She came willingly, her fear fleeing in a rush of hope.

* * * *

"All tests passed with one hundred percent accuracy." Petrosyan, the engineer in charge of the team that had been tasked with repairing Alek, smiled at Lillian.

She blew out a gust of air. She'd trusted CyberServe's technical staff to fix the damage, and Alek had recovered most of his functions before they'd laid a circuit fuser on him, but there had been concern anyhow. Waiting twenty-four hours after the restored matrix was fully online to run the last diagnostics had been difficult.

"I'm back, baby," Alek drawled, imitating the main actor from a tele-vid they'd watched the night before. He earned chuckles and applause from the group.

"He's in the clear?" Lillian needed to hear it before she'd believe the worst was behind them.

"Haul this hunk of tin out of my lab, boss," Petrosyan growled with mock irritation. "He's taking up valuable space."

"Not an inch of me is constructed of tin. Only the finest metals grace this masterpiece." Grinning at their laughter, Alek stood from the chair as soon as they unplugged him from the diagnostics machinery. He shook hands with the team and thanked them for fixing the damage.

Lillian refused to settle for handshakes. She hugged the techs, each and every one. When she'd told the engineers Alek needed his matrix fully restored, not replaced, they hadn't blinked. No one had pointed out how much more sensible it would be to simply yank a broken computer core out and put a new processor in. To most, Alek was merely a mechanical contraption, after all.

Maybe Petrosyan guessed what was going through her mind, because he winked at her. "Engineers are a different breed, boss lady. We do better with machines than people."

After several more minutes of gratitude and the promise of a case of champagne, she was able to leave with Alek. When they reached her shuttle, she paused to close her eyes and lean against her seat's headrest.

"Lillian?"

"Just basking in having you back again. With me." She reached blindly, her eyes still closed, half-afraid if she opened them, she'd wake from a happy dream and find Alek hadn't been restored after all.

His hand folded over hers. "Back with you? You never left me. We were together the whole while."

Alek had fought against that, had told her to go home and get some real rest instead of sleeping in a chair next to the table where he'd lain while the repairs were ongoing. She hadn't been able to. Especially over the two days when his matrix had been removed, leaving his body empty of what made him Alek. Lillian had existed on coffee, sandwich deliveries, and too many newscasts about the Freedom League. Artemis Neera was in a criminal psychiatric facility, awaiting a trial that would probably result in long-term, if not permanent, incarceration.

When she wasn't drowning in the wall-to-wall coverage of the attack on her and CyberServe, Lillian fielded calls from Tosha, Mr. Michaels, and her friends. Everyone begged her to let them know what she needed and how they could help.

There'd been a call from Phoebe too. Instead of ignoring it and blocking her from making any further contact, Lillian had taken the call. While it remained to be seen if their friendship could be salvaged after Phoebe's copious and tearful apologies, Lillian took pride in the fact she hadn't erased the possibility.

Though she hated to, she tugged her hand free of Alek's and started the shuttle. "Let's go home."

Minutes later, they stepped into her condo. She toed off her loafers in the foyer. Alek did the same.

"Come sit with me in the living room?" she asked.

He eyed her warily. "This sounds serious."

"I suppose it is. Please?"

He followed her. She tugged him to join her on the sofa. They sat looking at each other as she gathered her thoughts.

"I can't promise I won't get scared. Or act temperamental or weird. Being in a serious relationship again...well, you know how I am. I want to apologize in advance for whatever nonsense I fling your way until I put my head on straight where we're concerned." She smiled hopefully.

He spoke carefully. "Does this mean you want me to stay? As your significant other? Your lover?"

"If you want it too. Okay, I want it even if you don't, but we both have to agree to it. I mean, I wouldn't force you, I want you to want to be with me...ah, shit. I suck at this."

She shook her head at the stream of babbling she'd fallen into. "I love you, Alek. I'm ready to try."

He pulled her onto his lap. Kissed her deeply. She clung to him, afraid and yet eager to discover what their future as a couple would hold.

When they parted, she smiled at him. "There's one more thing."

"As if I don't have enough." He squeezed her tight, alight with joy.

"A gesture of trust. I have to make it, and I received Tosha's okay. After all, you are technically CyberServe and Life Tech property."

His brows bunched together. "What are you talking about?"

"You can't guess? I'm making you your own man. You're a free cyborg, to live life as you choose. To be with those you choose...whether it's me or someone else down the line." She choked on those last words, but they had to be said. If she was going to go through with it, she'd do it right.

"Lillian." His eyes rounded with shock. "Are you sure?"

"Hell, no." She laughed, the sound hysterical. "But yes. I love you, and that means I can't control you. That means putting myself on the line for you, whatever the risk. All I can do is hope we work out."

"We will." There was no doubt in his tone, which calmed some of the jitters shivering her gut. "I love you with all my...matrix. And circuitry. And programming."

She laughed, but when he didn't join her, she quieted, wondering what was wrong.

He clutched her, as if fearing she'd run. "I know how comical that sounded. But you have to know I mean it. Even without a bill of sale or license to own me, I belong to you. Forever."

"That works both ways, Alek. There's no one else, flesh or machine, that I want to spend my life with."

His kiss sealed the deal. No matter how terrifying the prospect, she'd signed on for a relationship. Lillian was giving him her heart, and all she could do was hope he treated it gently.

The kiss ended, and his gaze, soft with love, took on a harder gleam. "Shall we celebrate in the manner we both prefer?"

Her mouth went dry in anticipation. "Yes, Sir," she whispered.

Chapter Seventeen

Alek cupped her jaw with one hand and fisted her hair with the other. He moved her into position, holding her prisoner for another kiss. Her master's kiss.

She'd expected a bruising, demanding embrace. His lips were firm on hers, but more teasing than brutal. His tongue licked between them until she opened for him.

He tasted her with languorous pleasure. Neither tender nor harsh. He explored, as if they'd never kissed before, as if this was his first taste of her. He kissed her as if he'd never stop.

Lillian's breath halted. Her nipples tightened. Excitement bubbled through her, and she grew wet. When he stopped, her vision had gone hazy.

He pulled at her tie, loosening it, then unraveling the knot. He undid the first button of her shirt. Then the next. Down, down, until he was able to pull the fabric free of her torso. Her bra followed.

Without speaking, he used the silvery gray length of her silk tie to bind her wrists together. Then he rubbed his thumb over her nipples until they were pointed peaks.

Alek continued to silently undress her. He pulled her trousers, panties, and socks off. She was naked on his lap. Vulnerable to his whims.

He stood and set her on her feet. He wrapped the loose end of the tie in his fist. Still not speaking, expecting obedience without commands, he led her out of the living room, down the hall, to the playroom.

He left her standing in the middle of the room while he walked to the shelves and the implements hanging on the wall. He returned with a spreader bar and cuffs.

He buckled the cuffs, soft rather than metal, around her ankles. Pushing her legs apart, he attached them to the bar, so she'd stay open for him.

He looked her over, still maintaining that eerie silence. The lack of speech made him more intimidating. Dangerous. His regard exerted an almost physical sensation wherever he looked. She trembled before him. Her lips quivered when he stared at them. Her nipples tightened under his regard. Her pussy slickened while he contemplated it.

He went to the shelves again. Another pair of cuffs, which he used to replace the tie. Then he bent and folded her over his shoulder. He carried her to a section of the room where chains hung from the ceiling. He attached her cuffs to them and pulled the links until she was on her toes. She couldn't move. Couldn't escape. He had control over her.

He circled her and inspected his fuck-slave. His heated stare absorbed her. He stopped behind her. A finger traced, running slowly from the base of her spine to the crevice of her ass. Then he brushed her ribs from the back, one by one. The outline of her shoulder blades. So lightly, his touch whispering over her.

He ran his thumbs over the dimples just over her ass. Then he stroked the creases between her buttocks and thighs. Down her legs, his palms warm on her calves, then circling her ankles. He moved around and ran his index fingers against her toes, as if tracing them on paper. Skimmed over her shins. Still so softly that her skin became sensitized and reached for every nuance of contact.

Up, up, stroking the tender flesh of her inner thighs. He brushed up the lines where her legs met her mound. The cup of her navel, the front of her ribcage, the lower curve of her heavy breasts. The hollows of her armpits and collarbone. Her jawline.

His gaze rested on her lips an instant before he took them. He was more demanding than before, but used the same care and exploration. Bound, suspended, Lillian had no choice but to submit to his possession. To wallow in his exciting attention. He kissed her until her lips were aching and swollen.

He covered her breasts with his hands. Warm. Proprietary. The rough pads of his thumbs circled her areolas. A sizzle of excitement raced to her cunt. He tugged on her nipples. Pinched. A jagged flash of lightning from his grip to her clit. Her breath caught, and he pressed another kiss on her while pinching harder. She whimpered, and he rolled her nipples roughly, shocking and exciting her. His mouth worked hers, his fingers alternating between gentleness and harshness, giving her no opportunity to separate pain from pleasure. Desire rose high within and melted her.

His palms flattened as they traveled down her ribs and belly, until his fingers probed her slit. He withdrew and watched her as he licked her wetness from the digits. Tasted her.

He came close again and reached for her pussy. Her open pussy, easily accessed because the bar spread her legs apart. He watched her face as he explored, searching and probing, investigating each crevice and fold with his too-knowing touch, from her clit to her ass. The minutes spun out, with Alek showing no intention of doing anything but playing with her. Lillian's breath heaved, and she trembled as he brought her very cells awake. Only through sheer will did she resist the urge to rut against his hand.

His attention focused on her clit. He refused to touch the hungry, swelling nub. Instead, he circled it, teasing her endlessly with that almost-there contact, until the throb of its need became an ache. She shuddered. Her restraint, usually so perfect, slipped. She groaned.

"Please…"

He stopped touching her, and she whimpered, ashamed of her disobedience. The openhanded spanking he gave her had little in common with punishment. It sank heat deep into her and tormented her with arousal worse than before. Her cries sang with yearning rather than pain.

Displeased with the results, he spanked her cunt. That hurt worse, but her arousal grew anyway.

When the discipline ended, his attention aimed at her breasts. He cupped a mound and held it up. "I've noticed how much other men like to look at you. At these. Some women too. Your breasts are gorgeous."

He was circling her nipple again. Perpetually tanned skin against her flushed breast. He brought sensation tumbling from nipple to crotch.

"I like playing with them. Feeling their weight in my hands. Making the tips stiff. Seeing you tremble while I enjoy them."

He did enjoy them. Now that she was his, now that she meant everything to him and returned his love, Alek had an appreciation for her bountiful tits. They jiggled enticingly when she moved without a bra and top. The few freckles that dusted their tops, the smooth, unbroken color of their undersides. Her nipples' responsiveness when he touched them as he was doing at that moment. Such eager little points, displaying her excitement. Her pulse quickened against his palm.

It was a shame about all those wasted months when he'd been merely an order-obeying machine, incapable of grasping how lucky he was to fulfill her fantasies of surrender. He was eager to make up for that. He had the opportunity to do so now. He was free to love her. Free to stay with her.

The realization brought on the not-always-welcome emotions that threatened so often to overwhelm him. Because his love was returned and Lillian had sworn to give their affair a real chance, they no longer terrified him.

As he'd said, their new relationship was due a celebration.

He bent to mouth a succulent breast. As he sucked on her flesh, he found her clit, wet and swollen. He rubbed its shaft, setting off quakes as she gasped. When he felt her pussy clench, he left the eager nub to stroke her folds. Her pelvis tilted to invite more attention. Probably unconsciously. Lillian was usually well-behaved, only moving when he told her too. Her eagerness for him fed a smug pride. He excited her.

He slapped her cunt for the misbehavior. She creamed in his hand. He shoved his finger into her. She jerked with a shocked little cry, and her pussy clenched. He carefully bit her nipple, and she tightened on his finger again.

Alek fingerfucked her slowly while moving to suck and bite her other nipple. His thumb lazily circled her clit. He felt her rising, as if by telepathy. Deep inside, tension was growing, unraveling her control. Desire burning hotter. Rapture threatening, ready to bowl her over.

He shoved a second finger in and took her, his thumb rubbing right over her clit. She shuddered, helplessly chained, her body stretched long, her legs spread, unable to stop him. Tremors shook her as she locked up stiff.

He bit harder than before. Pressed greater friction against her clit. Reached deep into her grasping core.

She went over. Her hips bucked as much as her bonds would allow. Her cries echoed in the room as she submitted to his demands. He continued to thrust and rub, insisting she grant him every mote of bliss before he stopped.

He released her breast to look at her, keeping his fingers buried within her velvet wetness. Her eyes had closed, and she hung limp from the ceiling chains. Her pussy flexed a few more times before quieting.

I love her so much.

He withdrew his fingers, and her eyes fluttered open. Nicely unfocused, her features soft as if she dreamed. Contented. Fulfilled at his hands.

Lillian was still floating from climax when Alek removed the spreader bar and unhooked her cuffed wrists from the chains. He rubbed her arms, coaxing circulation to pump in them once more while leaning her against his strong body.

He picked her up and draped her over his shoulder. He carried her across the room, his hand wedged between her legs. He played with her pussy as they went. He pushed into her, making her shudder. A wash of excitement left her unable to see where he was taking her.

She was heaved up and back, dropped onto a small bed covered with satin. The metal frame, headboard, and footboard were festooned with bindings of canvas straps, ropes, and chains…whatever suited his fancy for their play.

He gave her no opportunity to think about what he might be up to. He ignored the ties of the bed to cuff her wrists directly to the black spindles of the headboard. He sat on the edge and amused himself with her breasts until they were stiff and sore from his demands. His gaze took her in from head to toe and up again as he delighted and tormented her.

"Such a lovely servant," he said. "That perfect mouth needs something to do."

MINE TO KEEP

He crawled over her until he knelt over her face. He opened his pants to release his thick, engorged cock. Gripping the top of the headboard, he lowered his hips. Her lips, obediently parted for his pleasure, closed tight around his shaft as he forged within.

Velvet skin over steel. The throb of his skin fluids was a pulse against her tongue. And so incredibly hot as he pushed just to the point of waking her gag reflex and pulling out to the crown. In again. Pumping, fucking her mouth, going deeper so she was forced to swallow his flesh or choke.

She sucked on him, her tongue working over his cock when she wasn't swallowing it. He began holding still every few strokes, embedded to the groin while she strained to accept his girth down her throat. He rewarded her with a small spurt of cum from time to time.

"I smell your arousal," Alek said after several minutes. "Your scent tells me you adore sucking my cock. Spread your legs so I can enjoy more of it."

She did as she was told, her legs sliding over the satin slickness of the sheets. She was wet with the thrill of her helplessness, of his mastery. Even when he caught her by surprise with a sudden thrust that set her gagging, she thrilled to his control.

He slid out and traveled down her body, kissing and nipping along the way. He kept going until his shoulders settled between her thighs. His head lowered, and he licked from cunt to clit. The room spun as Lillian forgot how to breathe.

He spread her folds with his fingers, baring her. He closed his lips over her clit and sucked it ruthlessly. She shouted as rapture barreled through her.

There was no teasing. No playful manipulation. He sucked and rubbed his tongue all over her clit, sending climax stampeding in a matter of seconds. She would have bucked, but he held her thighs to the bed. He devoured her until a second, more powerful orgasm blew her apart. The maelstrom of bliss, so intense it was damned near painful, surged violently.

She groaned as the spasms eased. "What do you say?" he prodded.

"Thank you, Master."

"Very good. Now for more."

He went at her again, shoving two fingers deep within to rub the internal hotspot as he gobbled her clit. Lillian's surroundings eclipsed in a blast of blinding whiteness. Ecstasy heaved, and she was aware of nothing else for a long, long while.

When she returned, she was weak and trembling, unable to move. Because he'd demanded gratitude before, she slur-whispered, "Thank you, Master."

She was almost relieved when he stood up. She didn't think she could take anymore. She was a puddle after the quick, insane climaxes, incapable of stirring a muscle.

Alek stripped off his shirt, and she forgot how limp she was. She had enough presence of mind to wonder at how startling his wide chest appeared, gorgeous with carved pecs. Beneath that lay the bumpy definition of his abdomen. She'd seen him naked more often than she could count over the last year or so, but for some reason, he was more impressive than she remembered.

Because I saw him lifeless over the last few days? Or because I'm in an actual relationship with him now?

Either way, he was stunning, and she appreciated that she was with him. He became more astounding still when his trousers came off, displaying those chiseled thighs that framed his cock.

He wandered to a shelf, and she lost herself in watching his ass flex as he walked. She was so absorbed in his beauty that she failed to notice what he collected before he came over to her with a butterfly-shaped device with attached straps in his hands.

She whimpered as he wound the straps around her waist and thighs. He settled the jeweled butterfly over her overly sensitive clit. She didn't dare object, but she'd already come so hard…

"Knees up and out. Prepare to receive me," he ordered.

She obeyed. He pressed against her, his chest flattening her breasts. His cock nudged her pussy, drawn to its waiting sheath.

The butterfly came to life. It fluttered and hummed over her clit. Lillian's thighs tightened against Alek's hips, instinctively trying to come together to protect her against the vibrations that lit her anew. A cry escaped her as he held her legs apart, as he pinned her down and kept her from preventing what was to about to happen.

He thrust into her, deep and fast, giving her no opportunity to prepare. The pain was heady; the ecstasy doubly so. Orgasm convulsed her at once, rampaging so her pussy clutched his cock.

"Good girl," he grunted and pulled back. He shoved in again, more than before, stretching her, forcing her to yield to his thick length, filling her agonizingly.

He punished her with his shaft. He made her take him, over and over. His groin slapped against hers and added to the hurt, to the incredible bliss of his demands. The orgasm wasn't done, but she felt another waiting in the wings. She yanked against the cuffs, but there was no escape from his thick cock sending toe-curling friction throughout, nor from the insistent vibrations on her clit.

Her cunt pulled on him and tightened so his every movement galvanized nerves as never before. Her breath was staggered as desire arced higher, as greedy climax slid closer.

He stilled. He held up the vibrator's control and switched it off. Orgasm edged back, remaining close enough to drive her insane, but far enough so she couldn't have it.

She twisted inside. Her body begged for the next release. She wasn't allowed to plead. Even the whimper that escaped could earn discipline, depending on how he decided to react.

He watched her struggle, a slight smile ghosted over his lips. He leaned close so his scrutiny filled her vision. "Are you glad to have my cock in your pussy?"

"Yes, Master."

"Do you want another orgasm?"

"Please, Master."

"Do you trust me?"

Her breath caught, and she stared at him for several seconds. A curious warmth, nothing to do with sex, stirred within her. She tried the words, tasting them.

"I trust you."

He drew out and in again, lighting her with an erotic blaze. "Do you believe I love you?"

Less hesitation this time, perhaps only two seconds' worth. "I believe you."

Another, slow, lingering pump of his hips, drawing her taut. His regard was steady. "Do you believe you're the only woman I want? The only woman who matters to me?"

"I believe you."

She did. Maybe uncertainty would return in the days ahead, but at that moment, she had no doubt. Alek would stay. She had nothing to fear when it came to him.

He clicked the vibrator's control. It hummed stronger before, and his thrusts were quicker, more powerful. She screamed as he took her over the edge. The world ceased to be, but for his intent amber-eyed gaze and the invading cock that drove her to paradise.

He groaned as his shaft pulsed, feeding her with heat and pleasure. He continued to pump into her, extending her climax until she lay shaking from the final surges, until he'd spent the entirety of his passion. She lay beneath him, her pussy, ass, and thighs coated with wetness, marking her as his.

He uncuffed her and rolled so she lay on top of him. He remained inside her as they calmed, kissing in quiet celebration of their union…physical and otherwise.

"I love you."

"I love you too."

The End

Threatened and pursued, they have no business falling in love. So that's exactly what they do.

Coming later in 2022, the third installment of the CyberServed series, *Built to Last*:

Victor was a cyborg spy during the corporate wars that devastated Earth. Now he's a refitted demo model for CyberServe, spotlighting the services a repurposed cyborg can offer…in life and love. Suave, cultured, and fully realized as a sentient being, Victor has it all, except the love he wants for himself.

Amadis Dubois has played second fiddle to the powerful her entire life. Now she has the chance to prove to everyone and herself she has what it takes to lead. She accepts a humanitarian mission to bring desperately needed medical supplies to a disease-stricken space station. If she can pull off rescuing thousands of lives, she can finally move out of others' shadows.

Fending off the attentions of a lovelorn cyborg becomes a secondary concern when the captain of Amadis' ship dies suddenly, leaving her the only human on board. With her career-setting mission endangered, pirates and rebels threatening at every turn, she has to turn to Victor for assistance after trying to keep him at a distance. Between moments of fighting for her life, she's vulnerable to the numerous charms of the cyborg she has no business falling for.

Life and love hang in the balance for Amadis and Victor, with trouble at every turn. They can have it all, if they survive.

Read Chapter One now:

Amadis Dubois opened her eyes and wondered where the hell she was.

Maybe *hell* was the wrong idea. Her surroundings certainly didn't look like a place of punishment. Everything around Amadis was stark white, as pure as resonator crystal wafers.

She stared straight ahead for several seconds as her brain oriented itself. A window slanted off toward a blameless, blank wall...no, it was a ceiling. She was lying on a soft but supporting surface, on her back. Inside a padded capsule.

Another second elapsed, and she remembered. She was in a cryosleep chamber, on board the transport *Golden Ray*, headed to Space Station Nu on the ITCS's frontier. She was in charge of a mission to bring lifesaving supplies to Nu, which had been stricken with a flesh-eating virus that was overwhelming the station's medical staff.

The cryosleep chamber, as explained to her by the *Golden Ray's* captain, was set to awaken her a week before they reached Nu, a three-month journey from Amadis' home, Space Station Alpha.

Amadis stretched and yawned. A voice suddenly spoke up, startling her into a yelp. "Greetings, Amadis Dubois. This is the *Golden Ray's* automatic piloting system, which has been enabled on an emergency issue. Are you fully awake and functioning?"

Her first instinct was to snarl no, she wasn't functioning. She didn't function until two cups of coffee were sizzling through her veins, and she damned sure wasn't functioning fresh out of cryosleep.

Coffee or no, the word *emergency* revved her out of her just-woke-up stupor.

"Emergency? What emergency?"

"Captain LaFarge has collapsed on the bridge. This system detects no life signs from its commander."

"Shit!" Amadis clambered out of the capsule and hissed when her bare feet hit the ice-cold floor. "Shitshitshitshit!" she chanted as the room's chill dashed past her thin underclothes. She yanked off the electrodes adhered to her bare skin, and the monitors tracking her recently hibernating functions beeped a soft complaint before shutting down. She ignored them in favor of dancing against the burn of too-cold floor.

"Apologies for the room's temperature," the smooth electronic voice said in its irritatingly calm manner. "The emergency protocol didn't allow for the chamber to be warmed to comfortable levels before you were awakened."

Peeling the last electrode from her chest, Amadis swallowed against a heave in her gut. "Or the usual anti-nausea treatment?"

"Affirmative. You will find a portable-sized bin by the door as you exit should you need to vomit. To guide you most effectively, I will light the corridors you need to join Captain LaFarge on the bridge."

"Hell of a way to start my mission." The task she'd lobbied her boss Tosha Cameron so hard for.

Amadis grabbed the bin the system had told her of on her way out, reflecting how funny it was to be nauseous after three months of hibernation. Nutritional needs in cryosleep were minimal, but apparently necessary enough that something in her digestive tract rebelled after being brought back to consciousness. The feeding tube had been retracted prior to her awakening and the small incision healed.

The blinding whiteness of the cryo-room was left behind for the gentler illumination of the corridor beyond. If Amadis' eyes could have sighed in relief, they would have.

The rest of her was far from any respite, however. "How long ago did Captain LaFarge collapse?"

"Ten minutes."

Amadis had been brought up faster than the usual safety regulations would allow. But ten minutes was a lengthy stretch if a life was on the line. "There's no sign of response from her?"

"Ship's sensors can detect no respiration. Other functions, such as pulse or brain activity, are beyond my ability to measure."

Amadis forced herself to jog despite her stomach's complaints. Ahead of her, lights flickered on, showing her the way along the gray-paneled corridor. "Any signs of trouble before the captain...passed out?" She wasn't willing to say *died*.

"Nothing out of the normal as I understand it. However, this ship has never had the pleasure of Captain LaFarge's command before this trip, so I am unaware of what might have been unusual in her medical file."

"You don't have access to that?"

"Just regulation checkups. Her medical status was in proper order as of seven months prior to this trip."

"How much farther before I get to her?"

"The hatch at the end of this corridor opens to the bridge."

Swallowing against her rocking stomach, Amadis put on a burst of speed.

The door opened obligingly when she reached it, and she found herself in a rectangular space. There was an impression of video monitors, gauges, and lights both steady and flickering, but her attention immediately centered on the crumpled form on the floor.

"Captain LaFarge!" She leapt down from the raised floor that ran the edges of the bridge, ignoring the two steps to the lower surface. She knelt next to the still figure. The captain had fallen face down, curled into herself.

"Vital signs sensory equipment is located in the emergency medical hatch on the aft wall of the bridge."

Amadis' fingers were pressed to the captain's neck. She couldn't find a pulse. She stood and looked wildly at the walls. "Where?"

She happened to be looking at the back of the bridge when a small panel slid open. She ran up and yanked a metal container with a bright red cross emblazoned on it. She carried it to the motionless figure and opened it up.

"What am I looking for?" Despite being in charge of a medical rescue mission, Amadis had no such training. She was an executive assistant, not a doctor. The system should have activated one of the cyborgs that was part of the ship's cargo if it had wanted to save LaFarge.

Except it has no preferences on the matter of human lives. It has a program to carry out, and as mission leader, I was the go-to.

Amadis felt the anxiety that she was in over her head. Nevertheless, she picked up the chrome-sided box the system identified as the vital signs scanner and pressed the black button it told her to.

A small monitor flipped up from the scanner. A steady beep issued from it.

"Point the end of the scanner at the top of the captain's head and slowly wave it down her body to just below the chest. It is unnecessary to shift her position," the system advised in its polite tone. "Then press the black button again."

Amadis obeyed. When she'd completed the task, the monitor scrolled down a list that blazed in fluorescent green lettering:

MINE TO KEEP

Heart Rate: 0%
Respiratory Rate: 0%
Systolic Blood Pressure: 0%
Brain Activity: None Detected

And finally:

Patient Status: Dead

"Shit," Amadis groaned. "We're too late."

"This system records the death of Captain Theresa LaFarge at twenty-three hundred hours, seventeen minutes, three seconds, standard ITCS time. If you will transport the body to the Medical Department for an autopsy scan, the cause of death can be determined, the ITCS informed, and a valid death certificate issued."

The body. Amadis marveled that a woman alive minutes before had already been relegated to such a remote designation.

It was then that she gave up the battle with her guts. Fortunately, the bin she'd hauled from the cryochamber was right there to catch the small amount she brought up. A few seconds later, she pushed the receptacle away. She sat on the floor and studied her deceased companion.

"Her name was Theresa?"

"Affirmative."

"Family?"

"An elderly mother on Station Beta with whom she lived. No other family noted. Will you be transporting the body to the Medical Department now?"

"Do me a favor, okay? Continue to call her Captain LaFarge. Let's have a little respect for an officer and somebody's daughter."

"No offense was intended. The system will comply with its commanding officer's request."

Amadis frowned. "You mean I'm in charge of the ship now?"

"Affirmative. You are the only human alive on board, which places you in command as long as your orders do not constitute an attempt to deprive the ITCS of its property, namely the *Golden Ray*."

"Well, I asked to be put in charge. I guess I should have paid attention to that adage, 'be careful what you wish for,'" Amadis muttered. For the system's benefit, she raised her voice. "As for taking Captain LaFarge to the Medical Department, I doubt I can." LaFarge was a large woman. Very large. Apparently, the body contouring so many spent their money on hadn't been high on her priorities. Maybe she wasn't paid enough...especially if she had an elderly woman to care for. Regular contouring was expensive.

"Gurneys are available in the Medical Department. Do you believe you could lift Captain LaFarge onto a collapsed gurney?"

"Depends on how low it collapses. Maybe." Amadis' toned frame had nothing to do with contouring. She could have afforded it, but she enjoyed tough workouts that gave her real strength instead of the mere appearance of it. "I guess I have no choice but to try."

"Agreed. Decomposition will set in before this transport vessel can reach its destination or a return trip to Station Alpha, should that be your choice."

Amadis frowned at the disembodied voice. It hadn't occurred to her to wonder how early she'd been summoned from cryosleep until that moment. "Which is closer?"

"Station Nu is the nearest of docking options for offloading a deceased individual by a margin of thirty-six hours."

Amadis had studied the route and distances to various stations before the trip. "Wait. We're halfway there?"

"If Commander Dubois is referring to an approximate time rather than specific, that can be computed as correct. We are eighty-eight Terran days from Station Nu, slightly less than ninety-one from Station Alpha. Would you like to select a course now? Or confer with ITCS Flight Control?"

"Give me a second." Amadis rubbed her forehead and tried to order her thoughts.

Space Station Nu was in grave trouble. The flesh-eating virus had seemed contained until two months prior, raging despite aggressive quarantine protocols. When Amadis had left with a cyborg medical staff impervious to the disease, antibiotics to bring it under control, and printing machines to replace limbs amputated to keep victims from dying, it had been estimated the casualty rate would climb to fifty percent within another three months.

Even with an immediate heads-up, it would take the ITCS and Life Tech, the medical company that had sent the supplies, a few weeks to put together another emergency transport. Amadis knew the issues regarding shipping the materials intimately…she'd done the research herself. Many on Nu couldn't afford any delay. The fatalities and mutilations would be horrific if the equipment and medicine were postponed by even a week.

"Can this ship reach Nu without a captain?" she asked the system.

"The system is programmed to pilot a set course and dock at its designated berth without human input. The captain is required only in the case of unscheduled changes and diversions in our path."

"I have no intention of diverting course. We need to arrive at Nu as soon as possible."

"Automatic pilot can succeed, as long as the ship encounters no anti-ITCS rebels or pirates."

Worry tugged at Amadis. The frontier was dangerous, but Lafarge had been the only crew on the transport. The route was safeguarded. If the *Golden Ray* continued on its flight plan and the ITCS did its part in guarding the established route, she should be fine.

"As soon as we have the autopsy done, send the ITCS the relevant information as to Captain Lafarge's death. Also inform them that I'll be continuing on to Space Station Nu."

"Affirmative."

Amadis eyed the unfortunate captain, noting again her heft. She might be able to roll her onto the gurney...but maybe she should accept some help.

"Light my path to the bay where the cyborgs are stored. Uh, after I put on some clothes," she amended, realizing she was still clad in only a halter bra and panties.

Made in the USA
Columbia, SC
27 April 2022